'I know what a huge step this has been for you.' Linton tucked a stray curl behind her ear.

The light touch sent ribbons of wonder through Emily, both his actions and words bolstering her fledgling confidence. She realised that, despite her misgivings, telling Linton her story had actually helped her. Trusting him had been the best thing she'd done in four long years.

He was right. She had been hiding. She'd been holding back—holding back from life and keeping her attraction to him a secret. Scared of being a disappointment. But perhaps she didn't have to hide any more.

She gazed up at him, taking him in, glorying in the look of undisguised desire in his eyes. At that very moment she knew he wanted to kiss her.

And she had no objection at all.

Dear Reader

Writing two books set in Warragurra has been so much fun! The people who live in the Australian Outback are hard-working, loyal and resilient, and the Warragurra community shares all these attributes. With its hospital and flying doctors' base, the town has generated some of my favourite characters.

The first book, A WEDDING IN WARRAGURRA, told Kate and Baden's story. As I wrote it, Emily just appeared on the page. I quickly sent her off to work with Linton, the playboy doctor from the hospital, and right there and then they demanded I tell their story next. Being an obedient author, that is exactly what I did, and I really enjoyed writing THE PLAYBOY DOCTOR'S MARRIAGE PROPOSAL.

Everyone's best friend, Emily hides her pain behind baggy clothes and bright hair. Linton is a city doctor who has come to Warragurra for A&E experience. He never plans to settle down—marriage is for everyone else but him.

When Emily comes to work at the hospital life changes for both of them. Do opposites attract? Absolutely. And as much as Linton fights his attraction for a woman he considers to be so *not* his type, he finds himself drawn to her, and to her loving family, until he's forced to question everything he thought he held dear. Along the way Emily learns to demand her place in the world, and to fight for what she believes in.

I hope you enjoy Emily and Linton's story, as well as the cameo appearance of Kate and Baden.

Let me know what you think!

Fiona x
http://www.fionalowe.com

THE PLAYBOY DOCTOR'S MARRIAGE PROPOSAL

BY
FIONA LOWE

MILLS & BOON
Pure reading pleasure

All the characters in this book have no existence outside the imagination of the author, and have no relation whatsoever to anyone bearing the same name or names. They are not even distantly inspired by any individual known or unknown to the author, and all the incidents are pure invention.

First published in Great Britain 2008
Harlequin Mills & Boon Limited,
Eton House, 18-24 Paradise Road, Richmond, Surrey TW9 1SR

© Fiona Lowe 2008

ISBN: 978 0 263 86349 9

Set in Times Roman 10½ on 12¼ pt
03-0908-49609

Printed and bound in Spain
by Litografia Rosés, S.A., Barcelona

Always an avid reader, **Fiona Lowe** decided to combine her love of romance with her interest in all things medical, so writing Medical™ Romance was an obvious choice! She lives in a seaside town in southern Australia, where she juggles writing, reading, working and raising two gorgeous sons, with the support of her own real-life hero! You can visit Fiona's website at www.fionalowe.com

Recent titles by the same author:

A WEDDING IN WARRAGURRA
A WOMAN TO BELONG TO
THE FRENCH DOCTOR'S MIDWIFE BRIDE
THE SURGEON'S CHOSEN WIFE
HER MIRACLE BABY

To Heather—a young woman with a bright future
who joins me on philosophical ramblings and
enthusiastically provides help with A&E stories
plus advice on all things radiological!

And to Alison for her help with deciphering ECGs

CHAPTER ONE

THE med student gagged.

'Out!' Linton Gregory, emergency care specialist, vigorously thrust his left arm toward the door, his frustration rising. Using his right hand, he staunched the flow of blood pouring from the deep gash on his patient's scalp. 'And take deep breaths,' he added as an afterthought, softening his terse tone. The last thing he needed today on top of everything else was a fainting student.

Where was everyone? 'Karen,' he called out, breaking his own enforced rule of no yelling in A and E. 'Room two, please, now!' He ripped open a gauze pack. 'Johnno, stick your hand here.' He lifted his patient's hand to his head. 'Press hard.'

'Right-o, Doc, I know the drill.' Johnno gave a grimace.

Linton shone his penlight into the man's eyes, checking his pupils for reaction to light. The black discs contracted at the bright beam and enlarged when the light source was moved away. 'They look OK. Did you black out?'

'Don't remember.'

Linton sighed and started a head-injury chart. 'This is the fourth Saturday in two months you've been in here. It's time to think about hanging up your rugby boots.'

Johnno cleared his throat. 'Doc, now you're starting to sound like the wife.'

He shot the man an understanding look as the familiar ripple of relief trickled through him that he wasn't tied down, that he was blessedly single again. And he intended to stay that way. He raised his brows. 'And yet this time I agree with Donna. Your scalp is starting to look like a patchwork quilt.' He lifted the gauze gingerly, examining the ragged skin edges. 'You're going to need more stitches.'

'Linton?' A nurse popped her head around the half-open door.

'Karen.' He smiled his winning smile. 'Stellar nurse that you are, can you please organise a suture pack and ring X-Ray? Johnno's got another deep scalp laceration. Oh, and check up on the student—he left looking pretty green.'

Her brows drew together in consternation. 'I'd love to, Linton, but the ambulance service just radioed and they're bringing in a crushed arm, ETA five minutes. I've set up the resus room and now I'm chasing nursing staff. The roster is short and half the town is out at Bungarra Station for Debbie and Cameron's inaugural dune-buggy race.'

He swallowed the curse that rose to his lips. 'Keep pressing on that gauze, Johnno, and I'll send Donna in to sit with you until someone can stitch your head.' Three weeks ago his department had been like a slick, well-oiled machine. Now his charge nurse was on unexpected adoption leave and her second-in-charge was on her honeymoon with *his* registrar. Marriage was a lousy idea, even when it didn't actually involve him.

He stripped off his gloves. 'Ring Maternity, they're quiet, and get a nurse down from there to help us.'

'But we're still short—'

'We've got two medical students. Let's see if they've got what it takes.' He strode into the resus room as the screaming wail of an ambulance siren broke the languid peace of a Warragurra winter's Saturday afternoon, the volume quickly increasing, bringing their patient ever closer.

Linton flicked on the monitors and took a brief moment to savour the quiet of the room. In about thirty seconds organised chaos would explode when their patient arrived.

Anticipatory acid fizzed in his stomach. Emergency medicine meant total patient unpredictability and he usually thrived on every stimulating moment. But today he didn't have his reliable team and the random grouping of today's staff worried him.

Andrew, the senior paramedic, walked quickly into the room, ahead of the stretcher, his mouth a flat, grim line. 'Hey, Linton. If Jeremy Fallon is at the game, you'd better page him now.'

Linton nodded on hearing the orthopaedic surgeon's name. 'We've done that already.' He inclined his head. 'Anyone we know?'

Andrew nodded as a voice sounded behind him.

'Can we triage and talk at the same time? His pressure is lousy.'

A flash of colour accompanied the words and suddenly a petite woman with bright pink hair appeared behind the stretcher, her friendly smile for her colleagues struggling with concern for her patient. 'We need Haemaccel, his BP's seventy on not much.'

'Emily?' Delighted surprise thundered through Linton, unexpectedly warming a usually cold place under his ribs.

She grinned. 'I know, I belong in a Flying Doctors' plane rather than an ambulance, although today I don't belong in either.'

'Ben's lucky Emily was driving into town on her day off.' Andrew's voice wavered before he cleared his throat and spoke in his usual professional tones. 'Ben McCreedy, age twenty-one, right arm crushed by a truck. Analgesia administered in the field, patient conscious but drowsy.'

Linton sucked in his breath as he swung his stethoscope from around his neck and into his ears, checking his patient's heartbeat. Ben McCreedy was Warragurra's rugby union hero. He'd just been accepted into the national league and today was to have been his last local game.

The young man lay pallid and still on the stretcher, his legs and torso covered in a blanket. His right arm lay at a weird angle with a large tourniquet strapped high and close to his right shoulder.

'He's tachycardic. What's his estimated blood loss?' Linton snapped out the words, trying for professional detachment, something he found increasingly difficult the longer he worked in Warragurra.

'Too much.' Emily's almost whispered words held an unjust truth as she assisted Andrew with moving Ben from the stretcher onto the hospital trolley.

Two medical students sidled into the room. 'Um, Dr Gregory, is this where we should be?'

Linton rolled his eyes. *Give me strength.* 'Attach the patient to the cardiac monitor and start a fluid balance chart. Where's Sister Haigh?'

Jason, the student who'd almost fainted, looked nervously around him. 'She said to tell you that Maternity now has, um, three labouring women.'

'And?' Linton's hands tensed as he tried to keep his voice calm against a rising tide of apprehension.

'And…' He stared at his feet for a moment before raising his eyes. 'And she said I wasn't to stuff up because she had a croupy baby to deal with before she could get here.'

Linton suppressed the urge to throttle him. How was he supposed to run an emergency with two wet-behind-the-ears students?

He swung his head around to meet a questioning pair of grey eyes with strands of silver shimmering in their depths. Eyes that remained fixed on him while the rest of her body moved, including her hands which deftly readjusted the female student's misapplied cardiac-monitor dots.

He recognised that look. That 'no nonsense, you've got to be kidding me' look. Twice a year he spent a fortnight with the Flying Doctors, strengthening ties between that organisation and the Warragurra Base Hospital. Both times Emily had been his assigned flight nurse.

'Emily.' The young man on the stretcher lifted his head, his voice wobbly and anxious. 'Can you stay?'

Ben's words rocked through Linton. *What a brilliant idea.* Emily was just who he needed in this emergency. He turned on the full wattage of his trade-mark smile—the smile that melted the resolve of even the most hard-nosed women of the world. 'Emily, can you stay? It would help Ben and it would really help me.'

The faintest tinge of pink started to spread across her cheeks and she quickly ducked her head until she was level with her patient. 'I'm right here, Ben. I'm not going anywhere.'

Then she stood up, squared her shoulders and was instantly all business. 'Catheter to measure urine output and then set up for a central line?'

He grinned at her, nodding his agreement as relief rolled through him. For the first time today he had someone who knew what she was doing. He swung into action and organised the medical students. 'Patti, you take a set of base-line obs, Jason you'll be the runner.'

Andrew's pager sounded. 'I have to go.' He gave Ben's leg a squeeze, an unusual display of emotion from the experienced paramedic. 'You're in good hands, mate. Catch you later.'

The drowsy man didn't respond.

Linton rolled the blanket off Ben. 'Emily, any other injuries besides the arm?'

'Amazingly enough, I don't think so. I did a quick in-the-field check and his pelvis and chest seem to be fine.'

'We'll get him X-rayed just to confirm that. Now, let's see what we're dealing with here.' He removed the gauze from Ben's arm. Despite all his experience in trauma medicine, he involuntarily flinched and his gut recoiled. The young man's arm hung by a thread at mid upper arm. His shoulder was completely intact as was his hand but everything in between was a crushed and mangled mess.

'Exactly what happened here?' Linton forced his voice to sound matter-of-fact.

Ben shuddered. 'I was driving to the game down Ferguson Street.' His voice trailed off.

Emily finished his sentence. 'Ben had the window down and his elbow resting on the car door. A truck tried to squeeze between his car and a parked car.' Her luminous eyes shone with compassion.

'You *have* to save my arm, Linton.' The words flowed out as a desperate plea. 'I need two arms to play rugby.'

I can't save your arm. Linton caught Emily's concerned gaze as her pearly white teeth tugged anxiously at her bottom lip. Concern for Ben—she knew it looked impossible.

Concern for Linton—somehow she knew how tough he found it to end a young man's dream with five small words.

'BP sixty-five on forty, respirations twenty-eight and pulse one hundred and thirty.' Patti's voice interrupted, calling out the worrying numbers.

'The blood bank's sending up three units of packed cells and X-Ray is on its way.' Emily spoke and immediately snapped back to the brisk, in-control nurse she was known to be. 'Jason, go and get more ice so we can repack the arm.'

Linton knew Ben's body had been compensating for half an hour, pumping his limited blood supply to his vital organs. Now they were entering a real danger zone. 'What's his urine output like?'

Emily checked the collection bag that she'd attached to the catheter. 'Extremely low.' Her words held no comfort and were code for 'major risk of kidney failure'.

He immediately prioritised. 'Increase his oxygen. Emily, you take the blood gases and I'll insert a central line.' He flicked the Haemaccel onto full bore, the straw-coloured liquid yellow against the clear plastic tubing. 'Patti, ring the blood bank and tell them to hurry up.'

His pager beeped and he read the message. 'Jeremy's arrived in Theatre so as soon as the central line's in place, we'll transfer Ben upstairs.'

Emily ripped open a syringe and quickly attached the needle. The sharp, clean odour of the alcohol swab dominated the room as she prepared to insert the needle into Ben's groin and his femoral artery. 'Ben, mate, I just have to—'

Suddenly Ben's eyes rolled back in his head and the monitor started blaring.

'He's arrested.' Emily grabbed the bag and mask and thrust them at Patti. 'Hold his chin up and start bagging. I'll do compressions.' She scrambled up onto the trolley, her small hands compressing the broad chest of a man in his athletic prime. A man whose heart quivered, desperate for blood to pump.

'I'm in.' Linton checked the position in the jugular vein with the portable ultrasound then skilfully connected the central line to another bag of plasma expander. 'Now he's getting some circulating volume, let's hope his heart is happier. Stand clear.'

Emily jumped down off the trolley.

The moment her feet hit the floor and her hands went up in the air showing a space between her and the trolley, he pressed the button on the emergency defibrillator. A power surge discharged into Ben's body, along with a surge of hope. It was tragic enough, Ben losing an arm. He didn't need to lose his life as well.

Four sets of eyes fixed on the monitor, intently watching the green flat line slowly start to morph into a wobbly rhythm.

'Adrenaline?' Emily pulled open the drug drawer of the crash cart.

'Draw it up in case we need it but he's in sinus rhythm for the moment. Patti, put the oxygen mask back on. We're moving him up to Theatre *now*. That tourniquet is doing its job but there's a bleeder in there that needs to be tied off.' Linton flicked up the locks on the trolley wheels.

'I've got the ice and the blood.' Jason rushed back into the room.

'Take it with you and summon the lift to Theatre. We're right behind you.' He turned to Emily to give her instructions, but they died on his lips.

She'd already placed the portable defibrillator on the trolley and positioned herself behind Ben's head, the emergency mask and bag in her hand. Small furrows of concentration formed a line of mini-Vs on the bridge on her nose as she caught his gaze. 'Ready?'

It was uncanny how she could pre-empt him. She was on his wavelength every step of the way. 'Ready.'

As they rounded the corner he heard the lift ping. Jason held the doors open as they pushed the trolley inside. The silver-coloured doors slid closed, sealing them into a type of no-man's-land.

Heavy silence pervaded the lift. The medical students watched everything in wide-eyed awe. Emily's gaze stayed welded to the monitor as her fine fingers caressed Ben's hair in an almost unconscious manner.

A stab of something indefinable caught Linton in the solar plexus. He shifted his weight and breathed in deeply. Emily Tippett, with hair that changed colour weekly, her button nose with its smattering of freckles that some might describe as cute, her baggy clothing, which he assumed hid a nondescript figure, and her diminutive height, was so far removed from his image of an ideal woman that it would be almost laughable to find her attractive. He exhaled the unwelcome feeling.

But she's a damn good nurse. The doctor in him could only applaud that attribute.

The lift doors slid open. 'Let's roll.' Linton manoeuvred the stretcher out into the corridor. He spoke to the drowsy Ben, not totally sure the young man could hear him. 'Ben, you're going into Theatre now, mate, and Jeremy Fallon's going to do his best for you. You're in good hands.'

The young man nodded. His expression was hidden behind the oxygen mask but his eyes glowed with fear.

Emily squeezed Ben's left hand and then stepped back from the trolley as the theatre staff took over. A minute later the theatre doors slid shut, locking them on the outside.

'What do you think will happen?' Jason spoke the words no one had been prepared to voice in front of Ben.

'High upper arm amputation.'

They spoke at the same time, Emily's words rolling over his, her voice husky and soft.

An image of a late-night, smoky bar with a curvaceous singer draped in a long, silk dress, its folds clinging to every delicious curve, suddenly branded itself to his brain. He'd never noticed what an incredibly sexy voice she had. It was at odds with the rest of her.

He shook his head, removing the image, and focused squarely on his medical student. Warragurra was a teaching hospital and he had teaching responsibilities. 'The X-ray will determine if the arm can be reattached but due to the violence of the impact it's very unlikely. The humerus, radius and ulna will be pulp rather than bone.'

'So what's next?' For the very first time Jason showed some enthusiasm.

'Cleaning up.' Emily turned and pressed the lift call button.

'Cleaning up?' Jason sounded horrified. 'Don't the nurses do that?'

Linton suppressed a smile and silently counted down from five, anticipating the explosion. Every medical student made the same gaffe, the sensible ones only once.

Emily whirled around so fast she was a blur of pink. 'Actually, it's the nurses who supervise the *medical students* doing the cleaning. How else do you learn what is required in a resus room? How else do you learn where everything is kept so you can find it in an emergency?' She folded her arms. 'And if you're really lucky, if you manage to clean and tidy in a timely manner, you might just be allowed near a patient and graduate from running boy.'

Jason's pale face flushed bright red to the tips of his ears as his mulish expression battled with embarrassment.

Linton started to laugh. A great rolling laugh he couldn't

hold in. His eyes watered and his body ached. Emily was fantastic. Just the sort of nurse he'd welcome with open arms on his staff. *Just the sort of nurse you need.*

He ushered everyone into the lift and this time the silence was contemplative rather than anxiety charged. If Emily came to work in A and E, so many of his problems would be solved. He could go back to worrying about medicine rather than staff politics because she'd organise everyone and everything. She'd always done that during his rotations with the Flying Doctors. With the resident he'd arranged arriving soon, and with Emily on board, he might even get some time away from work. His fifty-two-year-old father, who had just jetted out after one of his unexpected visits, had accused him of being boring!

Yes, this plan would free him up so he could retrieve his badly missed social life.

Emily in charge would make life very easy.

He started to hum. For the first time in two tension-filled weeks he felt almost carefree. *She might say no.*

He instantly dismissed the traitorous thought. When it came to getting what he wanted he usually achieved it with a smile and some charm. The doors opened onto the ground floor. 'Right, you two,' he spoke to the medical students. 'You make a start clearing up the resus room.'

Emily started to follow them.

'Em, got a minute?' His hand automatically reached out to detain her, his fingers suddenly feeling hot as they brushed the surprisingly soft skin close to her elbow.

She spun round, breaking the contact, her expression questioning as she glanced at her watch. 'About one minute. Why?'

He leaned against the wall. 'Still the same Em, always in a hurry.' He smiled. 'I just wanted to say thank you.'

She twisted a strand of hair around her finger in an almost

embarrassed action before flicking her gaze straight at him with her friendly smile. 'Hey, no problem. It was a fun way to spend my day off.' She gave a self-deprecating laugh and shrugged. 'I could hardly walk away and leave you with Jason and Patti, now, could I?'

He spoke sincerely. 'I would have been in deep trouble if you had. You headed off a potential nightmare.'

'Thanks.' He caught a ripple of tiny movement as her shoulders rolled back slightly and her chin tilted a fraction higher as she absorbed his praise.

He flashed her a wide, cheeky smile. 'You said you had fun and we make a great team so how about you come and do it again, say, five days a week?'

The constant motion he associated with Emily suddenly stalled. For one brief and disconcerting moment, every part of her stilled.

Then she laughed, her eyes darkening to the colour of polished iron ore. 'You're such a tease, Linton. Back in February, you spent two weeks bragging to me about your "fabulous team". Where are they now?'

He sighed. 'Love, marriage, babies—the full catastrophe.' The words were supposed to have come out light and ironic. Instead, bitterness cloaked them.

Emily rolled back and forth on the heels of her tan cowboy boots, her brow creased in thought. 'So you're serious?'

He caught the interest reflected in her eyes. He almost had her. 'Absolutely. I'm offering you a twelve-month position of Unit Manager, aka Charge Nurse of A and E.'

Lacing her fingers, she breathed in deeply, her baggy rugby top catching against her breasts.

His gaze overrode his brain, taking control of its focus and sliding from her face to the stripes that hinted at breasts he'd never noticed before. Quickly realising what he was doing, he zoomed his vision back to her face.

Tilting her head to the side, she gave him a long, penetrating look, her eyes a study of diffuse emotion. 'It's an interesting offer.'

Yes! She was tempted to take it on. Life was good. He rubbed his hands together. 'Fantastic. I'll get HR to write up the contract and -'

'I don't think so, Linton.'

Her firm words sliced through his euphoria. 'But—'

'Thanks anyway for the thought.' She rolled her lips inwards and nodded her head slightly. 'So, I guess I'll see you around.' She turned and walked away.

The retreating sound of her cowboy boots on the linoleum vibrated through him. He wasn't used to 'no'. He didn't like 'no' at all.

CHAPTER TWO

THE strong and greasy aroma of shorn wool hung in the air as Emily vigorously swept the ancient floorboards of the shearing shed, the thump and swish of the broom soothing her jangled nerves.

Linton Gregory wanted her to work for him. For a second she hugged the delicious thought close.

No, Linton Gregory wants you to work *in his department for a year.* Note the difference.

Ever since she had been a little girl she'd come out to the shearing shed when she'd needed to think. Or to hide. With four brothers to contend with, that had been reasonably often. She'd come and lie in the softness of the offcuts of wool, stare up at the rough-hewn beams, count the tiny sparkles of sunlight that shone though the pinprick holes in the corrugated-iron roof and find a sense of peace.

Now she was all grown up and far too big to lie in the hessian wool bags, so she swept and quarrelled with herself. For the last hour she'd been caught in an argument loop.

His offer is pure expediency. Nothing personal.

And deep down she knew that. Which was why when he'd asked her to work in A and E, she'd said no. Working side by side with Linton had been hard enough twice a year for two weeks. Working side by side five days a week for a year would completely do her in. She'd be an emotional basket case by the end of that time.

Her subconscious snorted. *And you're not now?*

She thumped the broom hard against the truth. She'd been a basket case from the first moment she'd laid eyes on Linton one year ago.

And she hated herself for it. She was twenty-five, for heaven's sake. A crush at fifteen was normal. At twenty it was forgivable. At twenty-five it was laughable in a tragic and pitying way.

Especially after everything she'd been through with Nathan. After that debacle, she'd promised herself she would never be that foolish again. She needed to keep her heart safe. But some promises seemed impossible to keep.

'Emily? You in there?' Her eldest brother's voice hailed her from outside.

She sighed. Her family knew her too well. If she'd really wanted to hide out she should have gone somewhere else. 'Yes, Mark, I'm here.'

'Thought you would be. You've got a visitor.'

She turned and leaned the broom up against the corrugated-iron wall and called out, 'OK, I'll come back to the house.'

'No need. We can talk here.'

She swung round, her heart pounding wildly like a runaway horse. Her brain immediately recognised that smooth, deep voice which held as many resonant tones as the colours of polished jarrah. Somehow she managed to halt the gasp of astonishment that rocked through her. He was the last person she'd expected. Linton had never visited her at home. In fact, he'd never visited her, full stop.

He leaned casually against the wall, all six feet two of him. His soft-soled Italian leather shoes had been silent against the worn boards more used to the firm tread of boots. His devastating smile hovered on his lips, tinged with the slightest uncertainty. But every other part of him controlled his space with magnetic charisma, from the tips of his blond-brown hair to the hem of his designer trousers.

Emily glanced down at her torn jeans and her brother's old and faded T-shirt, and groaned inwardly. At the best of times she felt frumpy and gauche, but she was usually in her Flying Doctor's uniform rather than her hide-from-the-world, comfort clothes.

She tugged at her hair and pasted a welcoming country smile on her face. 'Linton! What a surprise. What brings you out to Woollara Station?'

He pushed off the wall, toned muscles tensing and relaxing, propelling him forward toward her in one continuous, smooth movement. His lips curved upward into a full smile. 'I came to talk to *you*.'

His words rolled over her like warm caramel sauce—sweet and hot, fanning the bone-deep heat that had smouldered inside her from the first moment she'd met him. The ever-familiar wave of warmth hit her, spinning her round before dumping her against the shore, battering every one of her good intentions to stay immune to him.

She fought her dangerous attraction like she always did, using one of a cache of weapons in her arsenal. She dragged in a long, deep breath. Experience had taught her that men didn't find her attractive, and no way was she going to subject herself to excruciating embarrassment where Linton was concerned. He had *no* idea she had the world's worst crush on him and he *never* would. To him she was just a nurse and a mate—someone to chat to when no tall, gorgeous supermodel types were around.

That wasn't often.

Tall, willowy women flocked to Linton like moths to a flame. They came from all over the town and the region and the rest of the state. Visitors from Sydney often arrived for a weekend so he was never short of company. He dated a different woman every month.

I came to talk to you. Tamping down her reaction to him, she sternly reminded herself that his natural charm and emphasis on the well-placed words wasn't personal. She climbed up onto the post rail of one of the sheep pens and stared straight at him, her chin slightly tilted. 'So, isn't your phone working?'

He rubbed his jaw, his fingertips dipping as they crossed the cute dimple-like cleft that scored his chin. 'My phone's working fine, why?'

She balanced herself with her hands, gripping the rail. 'It's just you've never been out here before and it's a long drive on the off-chance I'd be here.'

He climbed up next to her. 'I wanted to talk to you in person. You raced off so fast this afternoon we didn't have a chance to discuss things fully.'

His familiar and special scent of sunshine, soap and one hundred per cent healthy man enveloped her. She gripped the rail more firmly so she wouldn't move away.

So she wouldn't move closer.

She surreptitiously shot him a sideways glance from under her fringe, taking in how his hair brushed the tips of his ears. Funny, usually his hairstyle was immaculate. 'I didn't think we had anything more to discuss.'

He slapped his thigh, indignation radiating from him. 'Yes we did! I offered you a job.'

'And I said, no, thank you.' Her fingers gripped the wood so hard they started to go numb.

'But why?' Genuine confusion vibrated through his voice. He sounded like a child who couldn't work out why the other kid wouldn't come out to play. 'It would be great experience for you.'

'I'd miss flying.' She tried to keep her tone light. She couldn't tell him the truth. That working with him every day would be delicious yet soul-destroying torture.

'It's *only* for a year.' Lack of understanding stamped itself all over him.

Only for a year. That was so easy for him to say. But for her it was fifty-two weeks, three hundred and sixty-five days, eight thousand, seven hundred and sixty hours. She stared at her feet. 'I don't want to lose my job with the Flying Doctors.'

'You wouldn't.'

She pivoted back to face him, her balance tested. 'How can you be so sure? I can't just leave for a year and expect to return to the same position.'

'What if you could?' His jade eyes usually so full of flirtatious fun, suddenly became serious.

A ripple of apprehension skated through her. Linton Gregory didn't do 'serious' all that often. 'The chief wouldn't be happy. He's already sent Doug Johnston to Muttawindi and now with Kate and Baden married I imagine maternity leave will loom pretty quickly. So me leaving would send the chief into a hypertensive fit.'

She jumped down off the rail, needing to put some more distance between them. 'Besides, this is all hypothetical because we can't even ask him until he gets back from the annual conference. You need help now. An agency from Adelaide or Sydney could supply you with an experienced nurse tomorrow.'

'Oh, come on. Now you're living in fantasyland.' Grumpiness and fatigue rode on the words. 'The Flying

Doctors attract staff because of the history of the organisation, the planes and a sense of adventure.' He sighed and rubbed the back of his neck. 'But Warragurra Base is a little more prosaic.'

She chased a tuft of wool with the point of her boot. 'But it attracted you. You came up from Sydney.'

'I did, but it's part of my career plan. I'm not staying for ever. One more year and I'll be back in the big smoke, sailing on the harbour.'

An irrational jolt of pain shot through her. It was crazy, especially when she knew he didn't really belong in Warragurra.

He jumped down from the rail and walked toward her, his gait relaxed. 'But this conversation's not about me, it's about you. I've spoken to the chief and he sends his regards.'

Her head shot up, taking in the high cheekbones, the smiling lines around his eyes and his cat-that-ate-the-cream grin. Apprehension exploded into full-blown panic. She'd forgotten that Linton thrived on getting his own way.

He leaned one arm against a beam. 'The chief agrees with me that a year in A and E will be a fabulous way to use your health promotion skills and it will hone your emergency skills.'

Her stomach clenched as her tenuous grip on control disappeared from under her. Anger spluttered to life. 'My emergency skills don't need honing.'

'True, but A and E is a different level. The chief thinks you will bring back more than they will lose by letting you go for a year. When you return, you'll return to a promotion.'

She stamped her foot as frustration swamped her. What was it about men just taking over? Her father and brothers did this to her all the time and she hated it. 'And what if I just don't want to work with you?'

His handsome face broke into deep creases and his chest started to heave as deep, reverberating laughter rocked him.

She summoned every angry, indignant fibre of her being and tried to pierce his self-satisfied aura with a withering look. 'I'm glad your self-esteem is so well fortified.'

He wiped a laughter tear from his eye. 'Oh, now, Emily, be fair. The few times we've worked together we've done exceptionally well. Hey, I even let you boss me around sometimes and I can count on half a hand the people I've allowed to do that.'

They *did* work together well. She hated it that he'd recognised that. It gave her one less argument to cement her case. She tried not to slump against the wall as she bent her leg and pressed the sole of her foot into a groove.

He causally leaned over a rail, his chin resting on his fist. 'And then there's your Master's.'

Her mouth went dry. 'What do you know about my Master's?'

His eyes flickered for the briefest moment. 'Don't you remember? Last year when we had to sit out that dust storm you told me you wanted to do your Master's in emergency nursing, but with Kate being away you'd put it on hold.'

Her blood dropped to her feet. He'd actually listened. Listened and remembered. It was completely unexpected—Nathan had never listened, it had always been all about him. She shrugged. 'It was just a pie-in-the-sky idea.'

He clicked his tongue. 'It shouldn't be.' He gave her a sly look. 'Warragurra Base would be the perfect place for you to work while you undertook your Master's.'

Her brain tried to keep up. Every time she had an argument he neatly countered it with almost effortless ease. But right now he was playing dirty pool. He knew she desperately wanted to do her Master's and that as much as the chief and the Flying Doctors supported the idea in principle, with the way staffing had been lately, it hadn't been possible.

Achieving her Master's would mean career security, senior positions and a higher salary. And she'd need that as, unlike her friends, she wouldn't ever be in the position of sharing income with a loving partner. Study leave hovered over her like the devil tempting her into his lair. Was this an opportunity she could really afford to pass up?

Linton pushed off the rail, walking round to lean his back against the wall so he stood next to her.

His heat slammed into her, dissolving all coherent thought. Emily breathed deeply, forcing air into her constricted lungs, in the hope her brain would soon get the much needed oxygen. *Think*.

She tried to fortify her resolution. Working at Warragurra Base meant working with Linton. Unrequited love from a distance had been tormenting enough. Up close and personal it would be torture. But still her words rushed out unchecked. 'How much study leave?'

White, even teeth flashed at her. 'What about you work a nine-day fortnight? The hospital will pay you for two days a month study leave.'

She narrowed her eyes. If she was selling out she should at least get a good deal. 'And one week to attend the "on campus" study component?'

He arched one brown eyebrow and tapped his top lip with his forefinger. 'As long as you can work it so the roster isn't short.'

She hugged her arms across her tightening chest as she committed herself to a path she'd told herself she'd never take. 'I can do that.'

He crossed his arms, his biceps straining against the soft cotton of his sleeves. 'Then we have a deal.'

Deal. The word boomed in her head over and over like the low bass of heavy metal. *What have you just done?* She silenced the words. Her decision was a career move. Linton would eventually leave town and she would get over her crush. Life would go on and she would have extra qualifications. 'A deal? I guess we do.' Somehow she managed to squeak the words out.

He grinned and leaned sideways, nudging her with his shoulder. 'See, that wasn't so hard, was it?'

She looked up into a pair of emerald eyes full of satisfaction. And why not? He'd just solved his staffing problem. All was good in *his* world.

But she'd just taken out a loan on her soul for a chance to study. Unless she was careful, the repayments on the loan would be pieces of her heart.

Emily stared at herself in the mirror in the Warragurra Base Hospital locker room, adjusting to seeing herself in green. Gone were the navy trousers and blue shirt of the Flying Doctors uniform. In their place green scrubs hung baggily revealing nothing of the shape that lay underneath. Hiding the big breasts and the short waist.

You are so ugly. High school had been a nightmare.

University hadn't been much better. *Cover yourself up, you don't want to put people off their dinner.* Nathan's derisive words boomed in her head. The memory of his curled lip and scornful look wormed its way back into her thoughts despite her best intentions to never let him back into her life in any shape or form.

He'd been the one to put the final nails into any delusions she might have had about herself. She now knew for certain that her body wasn't worthy of being on show, so she hid it, avoiding further pain and protecting herself from the glances of men—scrutinising glances that immediately turned to pitying ones.

She tied the string of the shapeless, baggy green pants. It was better this way. Men no longer saw her as a woman and didn't seek her out, which was exactly what she wanted. Her heart, which had loved Nathan and been so badly trampled on, was now well protected.

She turned away from the mirror and spritzed on some perfume, one of the few feminine luxuries she allowed herself. As the only female growing up on a sheep and cattle station, surrounded by men, being a girl hadn't always been easy.

When she was working on the station she generally became 'one of the boys' and fitted in that way. She could shoot a mean game of pool, muster on horseback for a full day without getting saddle-sore and was known for her skill in coaxing difficult engines into life. Her father, brothers and the employees at Woollara had long forgotten she was a woman.

If she was everyone's mate at Woollara, she was all nurse at work. 'Professional, organised and reliable' were the words that always turned up on her performance reviews. At work she had a different 'uniform' from the cowboy boots and jeans she wore at the station. But it was a uniform, and it made her blend in with the other medical professionals and told the community she was a nurse. The role absorbed her and she gave herself to it, enjoying every moment.

The only part of her that really said 'Emily' was her perfume, although most people missed that. They thought the thing that defined her was her dyed hair. But her hair was just a ruse. Bright hair hid her pain. Bright caused people to look up rather than down and distracted them so she could avoid their scrutiny of her lack of attributes.

She ran some hair gel through her hair. She'd worn it spiky short for so long that its current length surprised her. It was still above her shoulders but long enough for the curls to come back and taunt her. She tried to tame them into place with the waxy product.

In celebration or commiseration of the new job—at this point she wasn't exactly certain which one it was—she'd dyed her hair purple. The mirror reflected purple hair and green scrubs. Hmm, the women's movement would be proud of her. Then again, others might think she was going to take up tennis at Wimbledon.

She nervously fingered the hem of her top and then tugged down hard before breathing in deeply. She spoke to the mirror. 'Right, Emily. You're the unit manager and working for Linton for better or worse. Linton only sees you as a nurse so you're safe and your heart is safe. You're a professional and all personal feelings get left on this side of the door.

'This is work. Work is your shield against his charm. Focus on the job. You can *do* this.' She pulled her name tag and security tag over her neck and spun round to face the door.

CHAPTER THREE

PUSHING open the door, Emily walked into her new department. Unlike the last time she'd been in A and E—when it had held an air of panic and unravelling control—today it seemed almost serene.

'Emily!' Karen waved at her, pausing with one hand on the curtains of cubicle two, the other hand holding a dish containing a syringe. 'It's so great to have you here. I'll see you at the desk in a few minutes.'

She waved and smiled at the warmth in the other nurse's greeting. She hoped Karen represented the rest of the nursing staff with her friendliness.

'Emily, you're finally here.' Linton spun round, his freshly starched white coat sitting square across his broad shoulders and his stethoscope draped casually around his neck. Unlike his informal clothes on Saturday, today he wore a blue and white pinstriped business shirt with a silk tie. Everything about him said, 'A doctor in charge of his department'.

Puffs of heat spiralled through her. How could one man look so devastatingly handsome perched casually on the edge of a desk?

'I am, I'm here.' Duh! Of course she was here. What happened to 'lovely to be here' or 'looking forward to working with the team'? So much for wowing him and everyone else with scintillating conversation.

He glanced at her name tag, which snuggled into the indentation under her breasts. 'Survived the admin orientation, I see?'

She laughed, remembering her long and excruciatingly dull morning. 'As long as I remember to fill out every form in triplicate, I should be fine. I sometimes think Admin believes patients should be in triplicate as well.' She glanced up at the patient board. It was pretty empty, only listing two patients in cubicles and no one in the resus room.

'It looks like I've got a nice quiet afternoon to settle in on my first day.'

'Of course. I especially arranged it to welcome you.' His tanned face creased into a sparkling smile, which travelled rapidly up his cheekbones and into his eyes. Twinkling eyes, the same aqua green as the water around the coral cays of the Pacific Ocean.

She wanted to stretch out and float lazily in his gaze, revelling in the emphasis he put on the word 'you'. But that was far too dangerous. *Keep it all business.* She flicked a recalcitrant curl out of her eye. 'Especially for me? Yeah, right, I'll remind you of that when it's frantic and I still don't know where everything is.'

He gave her a long, pensive look, which finished with one brow rising. 'Ah, Emily, for a moment I forgot you don't let me get away with anything.'

A trail of pain pricked her. Surely she hadn't offended him? But there was no way she could flirt with him. He saw flirting as a game. As it was, she was gripping the last vestiges of her self-esteem when it came to Linton, and that was one game she couldn't play.

Before she could speak he slid off the desk, rising to his feet, his height dwarfing her. 'Now, I think you've met almost everyone except for the night staff. You know Karen and you've met Jason and Patti. Our students are with us for three months, and as you worked out the other Saturday, they're in their first weeks. As well as you starting today, we have a new resident, Daniel, and an agency nurse, Jodie. She's on a six-week contract but if she's any good we're hoping she can stay longer.'

'That's a lot of new staff.' A flutter of panic vibrated in her stomach. 'When do Michael and Cathy get back from their honeymoon?'

He drew in a long breath and sighed. 'Another six weeks.'

She did the mental maths of the number of hours in the day over available staff. 'So the roster's still short?'

He grinned. 'Not as short as it was a week ago.'

'And that's supposed to reassure me?' She heard the rising inflection of her voice.

He gave her a playful thump on the shoulder, similar to the ones she received from her brothers on a regular basis. 'I told you I needed you here.' He turned away and started walking as if he knew she would follow.

Irritation at his highhandedness quelled her mounting panic. She cut off a quip and took three quick steps to catch up as he was already talking as if she was standing next to him.

'If I'm out of the department when a patient comes in, I want to be notified. If it's a straightforward case then you and Daniel can deal with it, but page me if you need me or if you believe Daniel needs me.' He gave her a knowing look.

'New resident-itis?'

His shoulders rose and fell. 'It's early days but I don't want him taking on something he can't handle.' He stopped walking as he reached his office door, his face suddenly clearing of the usual fun and flirty expressions that defined him. 'Emily, we're a team. Don't ever feel you have to cope on your own. I'm only ever a page or a phone call away.'

His sincerity washed through her, trickling under her defences like floodwaters squeezing through cracks in a levee. Her mind threatened to leap from work to studying how his eyelashes almost brushed his cheek when he blinked. *Stop reading more into this than exists. He's your boss and he'd be telling all new staff this.*

She forced her attention back to the job. 'What meetings are expected?'

He ushered her into his office and picked up a stack of folders from his desk. 'We have a weekly meeting to discuss medical and nursing issues but I have an open-door policy so, please, don't wait until Tuesdays at two to discuss something important. Honest and open communication is vital in a department like this.'

Honest and open. As long as it only pertained to work, she was off the hook. She couldn't work at Warragurra Base if he knew how she really felt about him. She was embarrassed enough by it. She didn't want to feel this way. She hated it that after everything she'd been through with Nathan, even though she knew she wasn't ready for another relationship, she couldn't control her body's reaction to Linton.

'Right, I promise I won't let anything fester.' She held out her arms. 'Are they for me?'

He winked. 'Just a bit of light reading. We're in the middle of a policy review.'

'Policy review?' A vision of reading long into the night popped into her brain. Not that she slept that well, with Linton always hovering in her dreams. 'Did you just happen to conveniently forget to tell me that when you were twisting my arm in the woolshed?'

His eyes widened in feigned outrage. 'Twisting your arm? I don't coerce my staff, Emily.' He dumped the folders into her outstretched arms. 'By the way, have you enrolled for your Master's?'

'That would be the arm-twisting Master's?' She clutched the folders to her chest.

His mouth twitched smugly. 'All I did was provide you with an opportunity to do something you've wanted to do for a while.' He lowered himself on the corner of his desk, his eyes full of curiosity, appraising her. 'So, which subject are you starting off with?'

Surprise hit her so hard she swayed on her feet. She stared back at his face, so unexpectedly full of genuine interest. She hadn't expected that. 'I, um, I'm starting off with "Interpersonal Relationships in the Clinical Environment".'

Otherwise known as how to survive working closely with a boss whose presence turns your mind to mush and your heart into a quivering mess.

He rubbed his chin in thought. 'That sounds meaty. There's lots of scope there on so many levels—patient-staff, staff-staff, patient-relative, relative-staff.'

His gaze settled back on her, unnerving her with its solicitude. The fun-loving charmer seemed to have taken a back seat. She'd never known him to take such an interest in her before. Her usual approach of friendly mockery didn't seem right. She managed to stammer out, 'I—I thought so.'

'In a high-octane environment like A and E it can be pretty fraught at times, which is why staff wellbeing is high on my agenda.' He walked her to the door. 'Let's do drinks at the end of the shift.'

She almost dropped the folders as blood rushed to her feet, making her fingers numb. *He's inviting you out for a drink.*

Not a good idea, Emily.

But common sense had no chance against the endorphin rush. All thoughts of staying detached and professional got swept away by the sheer joy that exploded inside her. Her feet wanted to happy dance and her hands wanted to high-five.

Stay cool and calm. 'That would—'

'Emily, Linton, you're needed,' Sally, the desk clerk, called them to Reception.

Jodie dashed past, holding two kidney dishes. 'Gastro in cubicles one, two, three and four.'

Emily picked up the histories and noted the patients all had the same surname. 'Looks like it's one family.' She handed out the histories. 'Jason, you and Patti share Mr Peterson and Jodie's in with Mrs Peterson. Get base-line obs and assess for dehydration.'

Linton took the remaining histories. 'You examine the teenager and then join me with the eight-year-old.' He shot her a cheeky grin. 'Your hair colour will convince him you're a clown and he'll relax while I'm inserting an IV.'

She rolled her eyes. 'Ha, ha, very funny. I think I just have my first example for my Master's of interpersonal relationships with staff and harassment.' She jokingly tapped his chest with her forefinger. 'Be nice or I might not help.'

She turned away and pushed open the curtain to see a fourteen-year-old boy heaving into a bowl, his ashen face beaded with sweat. 'David, I'm Emily.'

He fell back against the pillow, exhausted. 'I feel terrible.'

'You don't look too flash.' She picked up his wrist and her fingers quickly located his pulse, which beat thinly and rapidly under her fingertips. She pushed an observation chart under the metal clip of the folder and recorded his pulse, respirations, blood pressure and temperature. 'When did the vomiting start?'

'After lunch.' He flinched and gripped his stomach, pulling his legs up. 'Arrgh, it really hurts.' His quavering voice stripped away the usual teenage façade of bravado.

She hated seeing people in distress. 'I can give you something to help with the spasms but first I have to insert a drip, which means a needle in your arm.'

'Oh, man.'

She stroked his arm. 'It won't hurt as much as the cramps. Tell me, what did you eat for lunch?'

'Sausages and chops.' He grabbed the bowl again, gagging.

'Take long, slow deep breaths, it really helps.' Emily quickly primed the IV. 'When was the meat cooked?'

'Dad and I barbequed it and then we ate it straight away.'

She wrinkled her nose. 'I think I can smell the smoke from the fire on your clothes.'

'Yeah, it was an awesome bonfire. I'd been collecting the wood for a week.'

What was it about men, testosterone and fire? Her brothers loved nothing better than a midwinter bonfire. 'Was it a special occasion?'

He nodded weakly. 'Dad's birthday. Mum even bought coleslaw and potato salad.'

Wrapping the tourniquet around his arm, she kept mental notes of the food. 'Did you have cake?'

'Yeah, one of those mud cakes from the supermarket.'

Swabbing the inner aspect of his left arm she kept talking. 'Sounds like a lovely party.'

'It was, until we all started vomiting.' His arm stiffened as the needle slid into his vein.

'Sorry.' She whipped the trocar out of the cannula and attached the Hartmann's solution. 'Now I can get you something to lessen the nausea.'

David stiffened on the trolley, his eyes suddenly wide and large.

'What's wrong?'

He flushed bright pink. 'I need to go...now.'

'Right.' She grabbed a bedpan from under the trolley and helped him into position. 'Here's the bell, ring when you're done.' She backed out of the cubicle, feeling sorry for the boy who had left his dignity at the door.

'Emily, how's your patient?' Linton stood at the desk, writing up a drug chart.

'I've inserted a Hartmann's drip. Can I have a Maxalon order, please?' She slid her chart next to his.

'No problem.' His lean fingers gripped his silver pen as his almost illegible scrawl raced across the paper. 'So does he have diarrhoea, vomiting and stomach cramps?'

'Yes, all three, poor guy. He's pretty miserable. It sounds like a birthday party gone wrong.' She opened a syringe and assembled it, attaching it to the needle. 'David said his mum bought coleslaw and potato salad. Mayonnaise can harbour *E. coli* so I'm wondering if we should ring the health inspector to check out the deli.' She snapped open the ampoule of Maxalon.

'Good idea, and worth a phone call.' Linton rubbed his creased forehead. 'But if it was the deli we should have other people in with the same symptoms.'

'Unless the Petersons left their food out of the fridge and in the sun.' She confirmed the dose of the injection with Linton.

'It could be the meat.' He walked with her back toward the cubicle, his hands deep in his pockets.

'True, except that a dad and his son were barbequing.'

He arched a brow and stared down at her. 'Meaning?'

She ignored his supercilious look. 'Meaning most of the blokes I know tend to char the meat rather than undercooking it.'

'Now, there's a sexist statement for you. I'm sure you have to be on the lookout for those in your assignment of interpersonal relationships in the clinical environment.' He flashed her a challenging grin. 'I can shoot your gross generalisation down in flames. I happen to be a brilliant barbeque cook and one day I will prove it.'

The dizzy dancing that had been spinning inside her since his invitation to drinks expanded. She couldn't be imagining this. No, the signals were definitely there. He'd asked about her Master's, he'd mentioned drinks, and now a barbeque. There was no doubt about it, he wanted to spend some time with her.

She ducked around the corner and helped her patient off the bedpan before inviting Linton in with the injection. 'David, this is Dr Gregory.'

'Hey, David.' Linton extended his hand, treating the teenager like a young adult.

The patient put his hand out to grasp Linton's and suddenly stopped. He flicked his wrist, shaking his fingers.

'Is there a problem with your hand?' Linton turned David's palm over.

'My fingers feel numb and tingly, like my hands have gone to sleep.'

'Hands? Are both of them feeling like that?' Emily caught Linton's concerned gaze as her own unease increased a notch.

David nodded. 'Yeah, it feels really weird.'

Linton placed David's hand by his side. 'It could be from

all the vomiting. We're replacing the electrolytes you've lost and we're slowing down the vomiting with the medication. This should fix the tingling.' He adjusted the drip flow. 'We need to check on the rest of your family but ring the buzzer if you start to feel any more tingling, OK?'

David nodded wearily, not even raising his head from the pillow.

Emily tucked the blanket around him, made sure he could reach his buzzer and then followed Linton. 'I'll organise for bloods to be taken.'

'Good, but let's get everyone together and review the rest of the family first.'

Jason, Patti and Jodie all reported that their patients had similar symptoms after eating the same food.

'So it's an open and shut case of gastro, right?' Jason recorded some notes in his spiral bound notebook.

'Perhaps.' Linton tugged at his hair, his fingers trailing a path, making his blond tips almost stand on end as he walked back to check on the eight-year-old.

'Something's not quite right, is it?' Emily shared his niggling feeling of doubt.

His eyes reflected his apprehension. 'I just get the feeling that if I call it gastro, then that's just too easy. I think I'm missing something.' He ushered her through the curtain ahead of him.

Little Jade Peterson lay quietly sobbing, her chest rising and falling in shuddering grunts.

'Honey, does it hurt somewhere new?' Emily ducked down so she was at eye level with the little girl.

'No, but who's going to look after Towzer?'

Emily exchanged a questioning look with Linton.

He shrugged his shoulders, his expression blank.

'Who's Towzer, Jade?'

'My dog.' She sniffed violently.

Emily stroked the little girl's hair back behind her ear. 'I'm sure your dog will be fine and waiting for you when you go home.'

She shook her head sadly. 'But his tummy hurt too and he was sick.'

Linton bent down next to Emily, his vivid green eyes fixed on Jade's face. 'What did Towzwer eat?

She clutched her hospital teddy bear. 'He loves sausages but he stole a chop too and Dad got cross.'

The meat. The buzzer sounded. 'That's David.' Emily rose and walked quickly back to the cubicle.

Terror shone in the boy's eyes. 'My face feels all funny now. It's like pins and needles and it's really scary.'

'We're working on what's causing these symptoms. I'm going to take some blood and hopefully that will tell us something.' She gave him a reassuring smile and hoped her face didn't show how worried she really was.

Something weird and neurological was going on. She checked his pupils with her penlight. Both were equal and reacting. 'Can you squeeze my hands, David?'

He put his hands out toward her. Fear shot through her, making her gut lurch. His palms, which had been white before, now looked red and blistered, with flaking skin. If he'd burned himself, they would have known on arrival. Linton would have seen it earlier.

None of this made sense. 'I'll be right back, David.'

She stepped out of the cubicle, her mind racing, trying desperately to work out what was going on. She rushed back to Jade and almost collided with Linton as he opened the curtain. 'Oh, thank goodness you're here.'

He put his hands out to steady her. 'What's wrong? You're

white.' He gently steered her to one side. 'You haven't got gastro too, have you?'

She shook her head. 'I'm fine but David's palms are peeling as if they've come in contact with a corrosive substance. Everyone is getting sicker and sicker in front of our eyes. What do you think this is?'

He clicked his pen up and down, the sound reflecting his agitation before he shoved it back in his pocket. 'I wish I knew. We've got nausea, vomiting, stomach cramps, and the father has blood in his stools.' His forefinger flicked off the tip of each finger on his other hand as he listed each symptom.

'And facial numbness and tingling fingers.' A horrible thought speared her brain. 'It sounds like poison.'

He nodded, his expression grim. 'That is the conclusion I've come to. It matches up that it must have been the meat that was poisoned because the dog was sick as well. I'll call the police. Forget taking blood. Organise for a urine tox screen on everyone and get it to Pathology with an urgent request on it.' He spun round, abruptly calling over his shoulder as he walked away, 'Then organise for the whole family to be in one space. I want to talk to everyone together.'

She gave her staff their orders and ten minutes later, with the tests sent off to the lab, Jason and Patti soon had the trolleys in a square. Each family member lay on their trolley in the foetal position, legs drawn up against the severe stomach cramps, and groaning as each spasm hit.

'I know you're all feeling really ill, but I need you to concentrate on what we're saying.' Emily stood between the trolleys where Christine and Brian Peterson lay. 'Everyone, including the dog, ate the meat and everyone has similar symptoms. David and Brian are the most unwell but I'm guessing that's because they ate the most meat.'

She touched Christine's hand. 'Where did you buy the meat from, Mrs Peterson?'

The sick woman trembled. 'It was one of ours. Brian slaughtered it a month ago.'

'Have you eaten meat from that beast before?' Linton asked, his voice quiet and nonjudgmental.

'Yes, we have, and we've never been sick.' She twisted a hankie in her fingers. 'I defrosted it in the fridge, I did everything the same as normal.'

'The symptoms are leaning very strongly toward poisoning.' Linton's matter-of-fact voice broke the almost surreal news. 'We'll know as soon as the urine tests comes back but in the meantime would there be anyone who might want to hurt you in any way?'

The father of two gasped. 'No, no, no one we know would do such a thing.'

'I don't understand.' Christine gripped the side of the trolley for support, her voice trembling. 'It was supposed to be a special day for Brian. David did such a great job getting the bonfire ready.'

Dad and I barbequed. It was an awesome bonfire, I'd been collecting the wood for a week. Emily's hand shot out, gripping Linton's white, starched sleeve as the thought struck her. 'David, what sort of things were you burning on the fire?'

The teenager replied listlessly. 'Just wood and stuff that I found.'

Linton's eyes flashed his understanding as he immediately picked up on her line of thought. 'Was any of the wood stained green, like the pine they use in the car parks down by the river?'

'Maybe.' He gripped his stomach as another spasm hit.

Emily spoke softly. 'This is really, really important, David. We need you to think. Had any of the wood been treated?'

The boy looked anxiously between Emily and Linton. 'I…I did get some from the building site next door.'

Linton thumped his fist against his forehead. 'Copper-chrome-arsenate. You've barbequed your meat in arsenic vapours. That's what's causing all these symptoms.'

Stunned silence and shocked disbelief scored everyone's faces.

'Arsenic. Hell of a birthday present, son.' Brian grimaced in pain.

'I'm s-s-sorry, Dad.' David's voice quavered as tears filled his eyes. 'Are we going to die?'

'Not now that we know what we're treating.' Linton gave the boy's shoulder a reassuring squeeze.' He turned to Emily. 'We need dimercaprol up to five milligrams per kilogram by intramuscular injection. It acts as a chelator and the arsenic will bind with the drug so it can be removed from the system.'

'I'll ring Pharmacy now.' Emily turned to her staff. 'Jodie, Patti and Jason, attach everyone to a cardiac monitor and monitor urine output. You'll need to weigh each family member so we can work out the dose of dimercaprol. The rest of the nursing care plan is to provide symptomatic care. A cool sponge will help, as well as some refreshing mouth-wash.'

Her staff nodded their agreement and everyone attended to their tasks. By the end of the shift the Petersons had been transferred into the high dependency unit for close monitoring. Emily stifled a yawn as she wished the night staff a good shift.

'You can't say we didn't welcome you with a bang. Who would have thought of arsenic poisoning?' Linton leaned back on his chair, his hands clasped behind his head, his broad chest straining at his now rumpled shirt. 'Fabulous call, by the way. What made you associate the bonfire?'

His praise sent streaks of happiness though her. 'At the risk of being called sexist, I have four brothers. When they were younger they'd burn just about anything, and David reminded me of them. Lucky for us, Dad taught us what was toxic and what was safe so we avoided potential tragedies like today.'

'The Petersons are one lucky family.' He rose to his feet and gazed down at her. 'Ready for that drink?'

I've been ready for you to notice me for over a year. 'Sure, I'll just get changed and meet you in the foyer.' She walked to the locker room, somehow managing to control her feet which wanted to spin, twirl and tap their way there.

It had been an incredible first shift. From the moment she'd stepped into the department Linton had seemed different, as if he was interested in her as a person, not just as a nurse. And he'd asked her out for a drink. She hummed to herself as she quickly changed into her jeans and loose-fitting top. She sprayed some perfume onto her neck and wrists, and almost skipped down the corridor.

As she stepped into the foyer she heard Linton's deliciously deep, rumbling voice. 'It was a huge first day for you, Jodie, but you did a fantastic job. Are you up for A and E's traditional welcome drinks?'

'I think I deserve them.' Her girlish laugh tinkled in the quiet foyer. 'I hope every day isn't going to be like today.'

Emily stopped so fast her boots squeaked on the lino floor.

Jason and Patti pushed through the door on the opposite side of the foyer, both dressed in city black. 'We're ready.'

Emily's stomach rolled. She swallowed hard against the rising bile. *Drinks for new staff.*

Her blood pounded in her head, drowning out all coherent

thought. How could she have been so stupid? How could she have got it so very wrong?

You always get it wrong with men.

This wasn't 'drinks' as in 'I finally noticed you and let's go for drinks'. This was a general invitation for all new staff.

Staff wellbeing is high on my agenda. Linton's words sounded clearly in her head. Welcome drinks. A 'getting to know you' session—team bonding.

She wanted to curl up in a ball and hide. She'd misinterpreted professional team building for personal interest. She'd let her crazy and out-of-control feelings for Linton colour her judgement so much that she'd heard only what she'd wanted to hear. An image of her jabbing his chest with her finger came into her head. She'd even let her guard down and flirted with him.

Linton turned on hearing the squeal of her boots, his smile wide and welcoming. 'Emily, I thought I recognised the sound of your boots.'

Like a rabbit caught in a spotlight, she had nowhere to run and nowhere to hide. *Be the friendly colleague and hide the pain.* Tossing her head, she forced down every particle of disappointment and embarrassment, and summoned up, from the aching depths of her soul, 'bright and breezy, Emily, everyone's best friend'. The public Emily that shielded the real her.

She walked toward the group, smiling. 'Come on, you lot. It's not often Linton opens his wallet so let's take advantage while we can.'

She linked arms with the med students and tugged them forward. 'Linton, I hope you've been to the bank. I'm not only thirsty, but I'm completely starving.' She flashed him a wide, friendly grin as she walked past. A grin that hid more than it displayed. A grin that made her cheeks ache. It was going to be a long evening.

And an impossibly difficult year.

CHAPTER FOUR

LINTON gazed out at the brilliant winter sunset lighting up the rich red soil of the outback and silhouetting the now still windmill against the backdrop of an orange sky. The beams of light caressed the earth, deepening and enhancing the already vivid colours. Nature's slideshow was a lot more interesting than the slideshow he was preparing for the hospital board meeting.

A flash of pink, white and grey swooped past, accompanied by a cacophony of raucous sound. The flock of galahs settled into the huge gumtree on the edge of his garden for their nightly rest. He hadn't used his alarm since arriving in Warragurra. The birds woke him daily at dawn. Somehow their early morning song seemed more acceptable than the grinding and bumps of the rubbish trucks and the antics of the late-night drunks that had woken him in Sydney.

He'd miss the birds when he left Warragurra.

Still, that wasn't for while yet. He headed back inside to his laptop. He'd ducked home to get some uninterrupted time to work on his report. Amazingly, his pager had stayed quiet and he really should have achieved more than he had.

Actually, the quiet pager wasn't all that amazing. Emily had been on duty today. In two short weeks she'd put the wheels back on A and E and his department was running even better than before.

Warm and cosy smugness cuddled up to him, stroking his ego. Talking Emily into taking the unit manager position had been a stroke of pure brilliance. She was the most amazing nurse he'd ever worked with. She only called him in when it was absolutely necessary and if it wasn't an emergency case, but a consult for Daniel, then by the time he arrived all the preliminary tests had been done and everything was waiting for him.

Somehow she'd even managed to whip some enthusiasm into Jason, who no longer sat back but showed signs of being proactive. She'd also cracked the cone of silence that had initially surrounded Patti. The department positively purred.

He had what he wanted—a reliable and dependable team and a department that met every challenge ably and well prepared. Life was good.

He stared back at the computer screen, rereading the same words he'd written over half an hour ago.

So if he had everything sorted at work, why the hell was he constantly thinking about Emily instead of this report? All afternoon she'd slipped in and out of his mind, which was crazy because he'd employed her so he didn't have to think about work twenty-four seven. But snapshot images of her would catch him unawares, like her teasing smile, the way her hips rolled and swayed when she walked quickly through the department, and the floaty trail of her very feminine floral perfume, which had an unexpected kick of sensual spice.

Emily and *sensual* didn't belong in the same sentence. Emily was a colleague and a friend. Yet just lately he'd noticed things about her he'd never seen before. Like yesterday, when she'd bent over to pick up a pen and her scrubs had pulled across pert and curved buttocks he hadn't known existed. He'd found himself wondering what else lay hidden beneath her baggy clothing.

It was ridiculous. Emily was the exact opposite of what he looked for in a woman. Tall, long-legged women caught his eye. Not short women with psychedelic hair. It must be a delayed reaction to his recent lack of a social life. Work had been frantic and he hadn't been out much lately.

The bold ringtone of a 1950s telephone severed the thought. He punched the answer button on his mobile. 'Linton Gregory.'

'Lin, darling. I'm here to rescue you from small-town life and small-town people. Let's fly to Sydney for dinner.'

His mouth curved into a smile at the breathy and cajoling voice at the other end of the line. Tall, blonde and beautiful, Penelope Grainger divided her time between her parents' enormous cattle station and the bright lights of Sydney, doing not much else other than enjoying life. He'd met her at a charity polo match a few months ago and had quickly discovered she was the female version of himself. No strings, all fun, and a well-honed 'don't call me, I'll call you policy'.

It suited him perfectly.

Since the nightmare of Tamara he'd been vigilant and had adhered like superglue to that same policy. He didn't need another I-told-you-so lecture from his father. *Date and move on, son. Don't get trapped again.* Hell, he should have listened better in the first place. It would have saved his heart from being ripped out, pulverised and returned to him on a platter, just like his father had predicted.

'Penelope, I would love to have dinner at Doyle's but I can't actually leave town this weekend as I'm on call.'

The pout of her mouth sounded in her voice. 'That's just

too boring. Well, I guess it will have to be dinner at the Royal, then. Can you meet me there at eight?'

'Eight it is.' He whistled softly as he hung up the phone. Work was sorted and his social life was returning to normal. A night with Penelope would put everything back into perspective and these strange and unsettling thoughts about Emily would recede.

Linton was early. He'd given up completely on the report, rationalising that a fresh mind tomorrow would be more efficient than trying to work on it tonight. Rather than pacing around the house like a caged lion, he'd showered and headed to the Royal.

The meticulously renovated Royal Hotel was Warragurra's tribute to the wealth that had once come out of the soil and had ridden on the sheep's back. One hundred years ago it would have been one of many similar establishments. But the mining boom had faded, wool no longer brought in the money it had and the other hotels had gone. With its intricate wrought-iron 'lace' veranda, the detailed mosaic floor in the foyer and the magnificent carved wooden staircase, the Royal had become *the* place to be seen and the social centre of Warragurra.

Its management had the happy knack of catering to all tastes, from the easy ambiance of the public bar to the rarefied atmosphere of the dining room. In the summer months there was casual dining on the heritage-listed veranda but tonight's cool and crisp winter outback evening had forced people inside.

He pushed open the door to the public bar. On a Friday night he was sure to meet someone he knew for a drink, which would pass the time until he had to meet Penelope in the dining room at eight.

'Linton.' A familiar voice and a waving arm hailed him as he stepped over the threshold.

'Baden, good to see you. But why are you in a bar, alone on a Friday night? Married bliss worn off already?' He shook the flying doctor's hand and signalled to the barman for a glass of merlot.

Baden shook his head, laughing. 'No fear, mate. Married life is pretty good. You might want to consider it one day.'

'I don't think so, Baden.' The familiar irritation chafed him. What was it about married couples that blinkered them to the idea that there *was* life outside being part of a couple? If they'd met his parents and seen their divorce carnage, they might not be quite so enthusiastic.

If they'd experienced Tamara's complete personality change once the wedding ring had slid onto her finger, they'd be rethinking the entire tradition. Words he'd thought he'd left behind trickled through his mind. *I hate you, Linton.*

Looking for a way to change the topic, he spied a gift-wrapped box with an enormous gold bow tied on the top, sitting on a stool next to Baden. 'Special day?'

Baden's blue eyes sparkled with enthusiasm. 'It's Kate's birthday week and Sasha has organised a surprise party for her. I have strict instructions to be in the dining room at seven-thirty with this present. Kate thinks I'm at the usual Flying Doctors' Friday night drinks and fundraising pool match. She's calling in to collect me after picking up Sash from swimming.'

Baden sipped his beer and chatted cheerfully. 'You might want to keep a low profile tonight. Most of the base is here and I'm not sure I should be seen talking to you, seeing as you poached our Emily.'

Linton grinned. 'You guys need to learn how to look after

your staff. All I did was offer her an opportunity to do her Master's. Besides, she'll be back with you in a year.' An unforeseen jag of discomfort suddenly snagged him under his ribs. He automatically rubbed the spot with his hand.

'Baden, you're up.'

Despite the noise of the crowd, the clink of the glasses and the pop and hiss of the open fire, Linton instantly recognised that mellow, husky voice.

He turned toward Emily and caught the moment she recognised him. Her hand gripped a pool cue, which she casually leaned on. Surely he imagined that ripple of tension whipping across her shoulders and down her arm before she gave him her usual broad, welcoming smile?

He didn't associate Emily with tension. She was a friendly, country girl through and through. She had no pretensions and was at ease with everyone, no matter who they were or where they came from. She was everybody's mate. His mate. The sister you could depend on.

She moved closer and her perfume encircled him, tempting his nostrils to breathe in more deeply. Making his gut kick as the sensual spice curled through him, sending heat spiralling. *Sisters don't wear perfume like that.*

'Hi, Linton.' She gave him a casual, cursory greeting and turned her attention back to Baden. 'It's your turn. The kitty's up to ten dollars.'

Baden's expression became apologetic. 'Sorry, Emily, I don't have time tonight, I'm meeting Kate in a minute.' He slid off the barstool and picked up the gift. 'Hey, Linton, how about you play for me?' A teasing smile streaked across his face. 'It gives you a chance to redeem yourself after the whipping Emily gave you at the pool table last time you were on rotation.'

He caught the shared laughing glance between Emily and Baden. He reacted in high dudgeon. 'I was being polite the last time I played.'

The glint of challenge sparked silver in Emily's grey eyes and she rolled her lush lips inward, as if she was stopping herself from laughing out loud. 'Polite? OK, if that's how you want to remember it.'

He caught the time on his watch. He still had half an hour before he had to meet Penelope. Half an hour to best Emily at pool and put her in her place. 'You're on.'

Baden's hand clapped his shoulder. 'Good luck.'

Emily sauntered to the pool table, chalked her cue and hooked his gaze with a shimmering dare-fuelled look. She then blew gently over the tip of the cue, sending a light smattering of blue powder fluttering into the air, like a nineteenth-century cowboy blowing powder from his gun. 'Seeing as you let me win last time, I'll let you break.'

He chalked his cue and stared straight back her while he blew the excess powder off the tip. 'Fair enough.' He grinned as her eyes widened and the cute freckles on her nose wrinkled. She'd expected him to be a gentleman and refuse. *Ah Emily, I hate to lose as much as you do.*

He lined the cue up with the triangle of balls. Bringing the cue smoothly through the L of his left hand, it connected firmly and precisely with the white ball, sending it cleanly into the centre of the pack. A loud clack echoed as the balls scattered, skimming across the green felt.

'Nice job.' Emily walked around the table, winding a strand of hair around her finger as she studied the lie of the scattered balls.

He bent over in a mock bow. 'Thank you.'

'Actually, I think I should be thanking you.' She smiled a

quiet, knowing smile laced with devilish glee before leaning over the table. She shot two balls into the right pocket.

He couldn't believe his eyes. 'Where did you learn how to do that?'

She spun around and grinned. 'I spent hours watching the shearers and my brothers. As the only girl growing up on a sheep and cattle station, there wasn't a lot of choice in the recreation. It was learn to play pool or spend even more time on my horse.'

'But you didn't just learn how to play, you perfected it into an art form.'

She had the decency to blush. 'Well, why play if you're not playing to win?'

He leaned in close, ready to tease her, and dropped his voice. 'Exactly.'

Her head snapped around so fast that her hair caressed his cheek, trailing her scent across his skin and tantalising his nostrils. He looked down into staring eyes as wide as pools of liquid silver.

Staring up at him. Staring into him.

His heart thumped hard in his chest, pounding blood into unexpected places. Disconcerted, he stepped back fast and turned toward the table, lining up the ball too quickly. Without pausing for breath, he took his turn and fluffed the shot completely. Frustration and disappointment collided and he steeled himself against the urge to thump his fist on the table. What had got into him?

'Bad luck.' Her tone of voice and expression held no sarcasm, only understanding from another sportsman who knew the frustrations of the game.

She bobbed down and squinted at the ball then stood and leaned over the table, supporting the cue. Her top rode up as she stretched out, exposing a taut behind hugged closely by blue denim.

His palms suddenly became damp and he gripped the cue. *Sportsman?* There was *nothing* manly about that derrière. Unlike the loose scrubs, the denim outlined with precision the perfect form that wiggled in front of him, screaming to be cupped by warm hands. His hands.

'Yes!' She squealed happily as another ball clattered into a pocket.

He groaned. What the hell was going on? He was being whipped at pool and he couldn't shift the image of her behind from his head. He gritted his teeth and swung his attention back to the green felt.

Emily walked to the other side of the table and faced him. As she leaned over again her shirt fell forward, exposing the rise of creamy skin and a touch of lace.

Both declared treasure below for the taking.

He breathed in way too fast and coughed.

Laughing, she glanced up from under her fringe. 'Old ploy, Gregory. You'll need to do better than that to distract me.' She hooked her gold necklace between her teeth, out of the way, and returned to the ball.

Hell, she had no idea that he'd caught his breath on a tantalising glimpse of breast and a hint of lace. Had he regressed to sixteen?

He rubbed the tension from his shoulder.

Her cue wobbled, hitting the ball on the side, missing its target but lining up the high balls for him.

'Damn!' She stood up and her baggy shirt resumed its normal place and all signs of treasure were hidden again.

Damn is right. He chalked his cue and threw her a superior 'big brother' type of look. The one he knew she hated because she'd told him once or ten times. 'Now let me show you how it's done.' He strode past her and took aim. 'That's one.' He moved to the end of the table and lined up again. 'That's two.' He glanced over at her to see how she was taking it.

She leaned casually against the side of the table with one hand in her back pocket, which pulled her shirt tight across her chest. He'd stake a bet she had no idea how sexy it made her look.

Sexy? This is Emily. Get a grip.

She rocked back and forth on her boot heels. 'Enjoying yourself?'

'Yep.' He grinned at her.

Her mouth twitched. 'You don't think you're celebrating just a tad too soon?'

'Nope.' He lined up the third ball.

He felt her warmth as she stepped up next to him and moved in close. 'You really think that will work for you?' The whispered words feather-stroked his ear.

He turned, laughing, his gaze fused with hers, catching a streak of pure good-natured banter. Pleasure unfurled deep within, streaming out to all parts of him, visiting uncharted places. 'Attempting to cast doubt in the mind of your competitor, are you? I thought you were better than that.'

She gave him a brazen smile. 'A girl has to try.'

But she had no idea how to try. Not a clue. If she did she'd be using her body the way most women did to get what they wanted. She'd waggle that cute behind and wear a low-cut shirt and distract him that way.

Just like Tamara had. She'd used her body as bait and reeled him in, hook, line and sinker. Then she'd had him for dinner, emotionally and financially.

But Emily wasn't Tamara. Far from it.

He'd only ever seen Emily in overly big uniforms or baggy casual gear. Tonight, for the first time, he'd more than glimpsed the surprisingly curvaceous body that nestled beneath. A body that deserved to be on show instead of hidden away under questionable clothing choices.

He'd always imagined she would have a dumpy body— the clothes she wore certainly gave that impression. But, truth be told, he'd never really imagined anything much about her until recently. Emily was Emily—great nurse, great fun, a mate, just like one of the boys.

The memory of her cleavage and cute behind lit up in his mind. *One of the boys? I don't think so.*

Emily, it seemed, was all woman. So why was she hiding herself?

'Hurry up!' She nudged him gently in the ribs with her elbow. 'A quick game's a good game.'

He peered down at her, using his height to humorously intimidate her. 'You want to be beaten quickly, do you? Get the pain over with sooner?'

'You are *so* dreaming.' Amusement danced across her cheeks.

He pocketed another ball. 'Is that so?'

She took a long look at the table and spun her forefinger around her necklace. 'I think your dream run is just about over, mate.'

He studied the lie of the balls. He hated to admit it, but she might be right. All the low balls had rolled close to the pockets. He picked up the cue bridge and put it in position.

'Tricky shot, that one.' She grinned unashamedly.

At a high angle he tapped the white ball gently. It clipped one of Emily's balls and tumbled into the pocket. 'Blast.' But the word lacked conviction. For some strange reason his usual desire to win had ebbed, and he didn't really mind that he'd missed the shot.

Now you get to watch her play. He shook away the foolish thought. 'Over to you.'

'Now let me show *you* how it's done.' She spun her cue in her hands and chuckled, a husky, vibrato sound that whipped around him, searing and sultry.

Heat slammed through him.

She put away ball after ball, looking up after each success, tossing him merciless smiles as her eyes sent silver lights cascading over him. The black eight disappeared with a thud.

He'd never enjoyed being beaten so much.

He got the balls ready for another game. 'This time you won't be so lucky.'

'Lin, darling, here you are.' Penelope wrinkled her nose as she picked her way through the crowd. 'I thought we were meeting in the dining room?' She tilted her cheek toward him for an expected kiss.

Hell. He'd completely forgotten about Penelope. He gave her a perfunctory kiss. 'Sorry, Pen. I was helping out Baden Tremont.'

She glanced around. 'Really?'

'Yes, and he did such a good job.' Emily's eyebrows shot to her hairline as her eyes crinkled in a smile. 'He just lost at pool.'

Penelope frowned and glanced between the two of them as if she was missing something. 'How is that doing well?'

'Ah, well, the loser has to donate twenty dollars to the Flying Doctors.'

Linton pulled out his wallet. 'Hey, you told Baden the kitty was ten dollars.'

Emily laid her cue on the table. 'True, but that's 'cos he's on staff. You're not and foreigners pay more.' Her stare challenged him to dispute her.

He knew she was making this up on the spot, but he was hardly going to complain seeing as the money was for a worthy cause. He tilted his head toward hers. 'Don't forget, you're a foreigner too now you've crossed to the dark side of Warragurra Base.' He pressed the orange bill into her hand.

She stilled for a brief moment and then laughed. 'Ah, but I'm on loan, remember. I'm not exclusively yours.'

Her fingers trailed along his palm as she curled her fingers around the note. A spark of tingling heat shot along his arm.

Penelope tugged at his sleeve. 'We need to go.' Her voice sounded unusually sharp.

'Enjoy your dinner.' Emily's friendly wishes sent Linton on his way.

'We will.' Penelope hooked her arm through his, her voice almost purring.

He glanced over his shoulder as they left the bar and saw Emily chatting vivaciously with Jason. His gut clenched. What the hell was going on with him tonight? He had a beautiful woman on his arm and an entertaining night ahead of him.

So why did he feel like he was walking away from something he'd miss?

CHAPTER FIVE

EMILY vigorously rubbed the whiteboard clean. 'Top job, everyone. We've cleared the place quickly today.' She smiled at Jason and Patti, who were starting to exhibit signs that one day they really would be good doctors. 'You can go for tea as soon as Jodie gets back.'

'Great.' Jason exchanged a look with Patti and turned back to face Emily. 'When we get back, will you have time to help us with suturing? We're in a bit of a mess with our foam arm.'

'Sure, give me a shout when you get back and we'll run over it. It can be confusing at first.'

'What can?' Linton appeared as if out of the blue, a pile of folders in his arms.

Emily turned and focused on smiling. At the same time she tried to settle the run of funny beats that her heart whipped off whenever she heard his voice. He had this habit of 'just appearing', and each time her already frayed nerves unravelled a bit more.

'Suturing can be tricky. Jason and Patti are after another demo. You're not looking too frantic.'

He tapped his folders. 'Sorry, I've got a meeting. Besides, they're better off with you.' He glanced over her head at the students. 'Emily's stitches are so neat she probably won cross-stitch awards at the Warragurra Show.'

Her adolescence flashed before her, absent of all girlish pursuits, no matter how much she might have longed for them. Her mother's death had left her in a male world, making being a girly-girl almost impossible. 'Now, that would be a snap gender judgement, Dr Gregory.' She neatened up a pile of notepads, lining up the corners and tapping the sides together. 'As a teenager I was too busy branding cattle and drenching sheep to be crocheting doilies.'

She shook her head and caught a glimpse of emerald eyes watching her carefully, their gaze questioning. She instantly realised that, instead of her tone being flippant and dismissive, the words had come out full of regret.

'My mother died when I was ten and Dad wasn't into crafts.' The words rushed out before she could stop them. Why had she felt the need to tell him that? She quickly cleared her throat and turned back to Jason and Patti. 'Right, then. I can see Jodie just walking in so you two shoo to tea.'

The students walked off and Emily continued to tidy up around Linton, who had perched himself in the middle of the desk. She could feel his stare on her.

He spoke softly. 'I'm sorry, I didn't realise you'd lost your mum at such a young age.'

She bit her lip and gave a brief nod, acknowledging that she'd heard him. She really didn't want to talk about this—not now in the middle of the A and E. She pulled open the filing cabinet. 'It's almost two o'clock, you'll be late for your meeting.'

'Are you pushing me out of my own department?' He grinned his easy, bone-melting smile.

Rivers of yearning rolled through her, pulling at every barricade she'd erected in her attempt to stay immune to him. *Immune.* What a joke.

But joking was part of her repertoire to stay strong. 'Yes, I'm pushing you out. Surely you knew when you hired me that I didn't like doctors cluttering up the place? We've no patients so you're not needed.'

He gave her a hangdog look. 'That's a bit harsh.'

She laughed. 'You should have thought of that before you bribed me to work here. Go to your meeting or you might just end up dusted and filed.'

His eyes darkened to a deep jade. 'That could be fun.'

The phone rang as her cheeks burned at his blatant flirting. She'd promised herself she wasn't going down that path but Linton made it all too easy to take the wrong road. As she picked up the phone she mouthed, 'Go,' and pointed to the door.

He tugged his forelock and walked out, whistling.

'A and E. Emily Tippett speaking.'

'Em, it's Trix Baxter.' The school nurse from Warragurra High School spoke down the line. 'I'm just pulling up outside now with Samantha Joseph. She sort of collapsed at netball and went over on her ankle. She might have blacked out but she needs to be checked out. Can you bring out a wheel-chair?'

'Be there in a sec, Trix.' Emily hung up the phone and walked toward the doors with a wheelchair.

She met a tall teenager coming toward her, hopping and leaning heavily on Trix's arm.

'I guess you must be Samantha. I'm Emily. Take a seat.' She put the brakes on the wheelchair.

Breathless and pale, Samantha grimaced and then lowered herself into the chair with Emily's help. 'Thanks.'

Trix frowned. 'Sorry, Emily, but I have to get back to school and we haven't been able to contact Sam's mother.'

Emily swung the wheelchair around. 'Don't worry. Leave all the contact details with Reception and they'll keep trying.'

'Thanks.' Trix bent down next to Samantha. 'Sam, they'll look after you here. I'm sure it's just a bad sprain but it's best to get it X-rayed.' She patted her arm.

'Thanks, Mrs Baxter.' The girl closed her eyes as if the effort to speak was almost too much.

'Let's get you inside and have a good look at this ankle.' Emily briskly pushed the wheelchair into A and E. 'What position were you playing?'

'Goal defence.' The girl's hands fidgeted in her lap.

Emily helped her up onto the trolley. 'We'll have to put you into one of those totally gorgeous hospital gowns for the X-ray.' She smiled, trying to relax the girl. 'But first of all we'll get you some ice for the ankle and some pain relief so that it won't hurt so much to get undressed.'

'OK.' She suddenly looked a lot younger than her fifteen years.

Emily quickly grabbed the blue sports-injury ice pack from the fridge, wrapped it in a towel and came back into the cubicle. 'I'll just put this on your ankle.' She rested her hand on the bottom of Sam's tracksuit pants and went to pull them up.

'Leave them, I'm cold.' Sam leaned forward, her hands sitting firmly on the hems of her pants, as if she didn't want the material slid up her leg. 'Can't the ice pack just sit on the top of my ankle?'

'Sure.' Emily put it in place, surprised at the sudden energy the previously lethargic girl showed.

'OK, now I need to do some observations. First your pulse.' She pulled her fob watch out of her pocket.

The girl stuck out her arm, her fine wrist looking ludicrously tiny peeking out of an oversized rugby top.

A rapid beat pulsed under Emily's fingers. She started counting. The fast throb jumped against her fingers. She frowned and continued counting. It jumped again. 'Sam, did you black out on the netball court?'

'Dunno.' She stared at the wall, avoiding Emily's eyes.

She probed gently, needing information but not wanting to upset the girl. 'Did you feel dizzy or light-headed?'

Sam spoke quickly. 'I think I just got bumped too hard.' Her left hand started to finger the edge of the blanket, a red rash on her fingertips obvious against the pale wool.

Emily's radar went on alert. Something odd was going on. She flicked on the cardiac monitor and sorted out the leads. 'We're going to have to put that hospital gown on a bit earlier than I thought, Sam.' She held up a packet of dots. 'I need to put these on your chest so I can see your heartbeat on the monitor.'

'I want to keep my own clothes on.' Sam's mouth pouted in displeasure.

'You can put your rugby top back on over the gown.' She helped the girl lean forward and assisted her in pulling the top over her head. The netball top came off with it.

Shock reverberated through every part of Emily as she worked to stall the gasp in her throat. Every rib of Sam's body pushed her thin skin out and her scapulas protruded. Not a trace of covering fat existed.

Acting as if she hadn't noticed, she quickly helped the girl's stick-like arms into the sleeves of the gown.

'I'm cold,' Sam complained.

'I'll have you warm in a minute and you can wear your jacket over the gown as well as being tucked up in a blanket.'

She quickly attached the dots, connected the leads and plugged in the monitor.

The ECG blipped reassuringly as each beat of the heart traced across the screen in bright green waves, showing a normal sinus rhythm.

Perhaps she'd imagined the irregular pulse. 'You can put your top back on now.' Emily turned the sleeves the right way round and passed it to her. The machine suddenly beeped rapidly.

'What's that?' Sam glanced anxiously at the monitor.

'Your heart just gave off an odd beat. 'Do you feel funny?'

'No.' Fear lit the young girl's eyes.

'Well, that's good, but I'm just going to get Dr Gregory to have a look at you.' She passed the buzzer. 'Call me if you need me but I'll be back in a minute.'

She strode quickly to the desk, picked up the phone and punched the number of Linton's mobile into the keypad.

He answered immediately, his crisp, professional voice reassuring her as well as giving her own heart some funny beats. She tried to sound equally crisp and professional. 'Linton, I've got a fifteen-year-old throwing off ectopic beats.'

He didn't hesitate. 'I'm on my way.'

Instantly, the phone went dead in her ear. She phoned Reception. 'Tracey, I need Samantha Joseph's history asap and have you got onto her parents yet?'

'I'm bringing the history round and we've left messages for the mother.' Tracey's efficiency made life in A and E much easier.

'Thanks, Trace.' She dropped the phone into the cradle and jogged into the supply room, picking up a saline drip and setting up an IV trolley.

'So you got rid of me too early, then?'

She swung around and caught Linton's teasing smile and flash of white teeth. 'So it seems. Samantha Joseph came in with a sprained ankle after collapsing at netball, but my concern is that she's throwing off a few extra heartbeats.' She pushed the trolley toward the door. 'Come and see what you think.'

Linton ushered her into the cubicle and greeted their patient. 'Hi, Samantha, I'm Linton Gregory, and I'm the doctor on duty today. Emily tells me you've been in the wars.' He smiled his golden smile. 'Tough game, netball.'

Samantha giggled and batted her eyelashes while her heart rate visibly leapt on the monitor.

Emily silently groaned. She knew her own heart rate did a similar thing when Linton smiled at her—the man charmed every woman in sight. It was what he did with effortless ease. She'd had to work so hard being casual and friendly to get Samantha to co-operate and all Linton had to do was smile.

'I just want to listen to your lungs so if you can pull up your top, I'll make sure the stethoscope's warmed up.'

'OK.'

Sam leaned forward with such unexpected compliance that Emily hardly recognised her as she helped her lift her top.

Shock, frustration and pity scored Linton's normal urbane face as he caught sight of Sam's desperately thin frame. He listened intently to her air entry, which Emily knew was really an excuse to examine her back and view the evidence that this girl was indeed starving.

He swung his stethoscope around his neck. 'That sounds fine. Now, what about this ankle?' He pushed up her track-suit pants and placed his large, tanned hands around her ankle, feeling for broken bones. But again Emily knew it was also a chance to examine her legs for signs of self-harm. 'I don't think you've broken it.'

He leaned his arms casually against the cot-side of the trolley and stared intently at the monitor.

'Coupled premature ventricular complex?' Emily wanted confirmation that she was actually seeing the paired abnormal beats, as there had been a long period since that last couplet.

Linton nodded slowly, his brow furrowed in thought. 'They're just occasional so we'll monitor her for now.'

He turned back to Sam. 'Your ankle will be fine. I'm actually more worried about the funny little beats of your heart.'

'Why would it be doing that?'

He breathed in deeply. 'That's what we want to find out. Emily's going to take some blood and put a drip in your arm.'

'Oh, are you going?' Sam's crestfallen expression radiated dismay.

'You can't get rid of me that easily.' He gave her an easy smile and pressed a button to print a readout from the monitor.

Sam caught sight of Emily opening the IV cannula onto the sterile field of the dressing pack. 'Will it hurt?'

He ripped the printout off the monitor. 'Nah, I'll keep my questions as painless as possible.'

Sam laughed and Emily slipped the tourniquet onto the girl's arm, tightening it to find a vein. Linton would keep Sam distracted while she took the blood.

Linton focused his attention back onto Sam. 'Have you been feeling sick lately?'

'A bit. I feel sick when I eat.' She glanced at Emily, who was swabbing her arm.

Linton nodded, his expression one of understanding. 'In the mornings or all day?'

'All day.'

'Have you been feeling sick for a long time?'

'A few months. Ouch!'

Emily released the tourniquet as she withdrew the trocar from the cannula. 'Sorry, but that's it. I've taken the blood and the IV is in.' She passed the blood vial to Jodie, who had arrived to run the specimen to the lab.

'Have you been eating much at all?' Linton stayed on task, chipping away.

The clack of high heels sounded on the floor. 'I want to see her now!'

Jodie's placating voice sounded in the distance and then the curtains moved and a well-dressed woman in a black suit appeared.

'Darling, are you all right?' The woman rushed to Sam's side and picked up her hand. Then she took in Emily and Linton. 'I'm Rachel, Sam's mum. What's wrong with her?'

'That's what we're trying to work out.' Linton continued smoothly, 'I was just wondering if Sam had been eating enough.'

Rachel sighed. 'She's like every teenage girl. She won't eat breakfast but she eats a good lunch and dinner, don't you, darling?' She stroked Sam's hair.

For the first time Sam dropped her gaze from Linton's but she didn't look at her mother. She mumbled, 'I eat enough.'

The monitor screeched as Sam's heart threw off a series of arrhythmias, the high line dipping low rather than soaring high. 'Ventricular tachycardia?' Anxiety fluttered in Emily's gut.

Linton's brow creased in a worried frown. 'Bigeminal PVCs. Give her two grams of potassium chloride in one hundred millilitres of saline over an hour through an infusion pump. Let's try and head ventricular tachycardia off at the pass.'

'What about lignocaine to soothe vein irritation?' Emily snapped open the ampoule of KCL.

'Good idea.' Linton wrote up the drug order.

'What's happening?' Rachel's distressed voice sounded loud in the small area.

'We think that Sam's very low on potassium and that's affecting her heart. It's causing the large chamber of her heart, the ventricle, to have these funny beats.' He pointed to the monitor showing the wider beats with the negative drops.

The mother's eyes widened in disbelief. 'Potassium? I don't understand. She's never had anything wrong with her heart.'

Emily injected the KCL into the burette and titrated the drip flow through the pump. She shot Linton a knowing look. Rachel had no idea about Sam's anorexia.

Linton put his hand on the scared girl's arm. 'I believe you when you say you eat enough.'

Sam's shoulders relaxed and she gave Linton a coy smile.

Linton's tone stayed gentle but firm. 'But your body is missing a lot of nutrients and you're very, very thin. So for us to help you, I need you to be honest with me. Have you been using laxatives so that what you eat gets quickly out of your body?'

Sam looked down, pulling at a loose thread on the blanket and unravelling the blanket stitch.

Rachel slumped into the chair by the trolley, still holding her daughter's hand. 'Honey, please, tell us. No one is going to get cross.'

Tears formed slowly and spilled down Sam's cheeks. 'I had to. You made me eat. I'm fat and this is the only way for me to be pretty.'

Emily's heart contracted in pain. Being pretty was everything at fifteen. The taunting voices of high school echoed in her mind. *Hey, Ranga! With that hair and those freckles, no guy will ever think you're hot.*

And they hadn't. She'd never dated until she'd gone to university and even then the only person to beat a path to her door had been Nathan.

He'd reinforced every taunt she'd tried to put behind her. A sigh shuddered through as the memory of Nathan's sarcastic eyes seared her soul, his snarling voice booming in her head. *You're not exactly model material, are you?*

She caught Linton staring at her, his gaze too intent for comfort and his frown disapproving. She immediately covered her reaction by checking the drip.

Linton blinked and turned toward Rachel. 'We're going to admit Samantha and get her electrolytes sorted out. Then we can discuss her ongoing care with regard to her anorexia, which will probably involve a transfer to Sydney.'

Rachel shook her head, as if the action would help her take in the situation. 'I didn't realise...'

Linton's sympathetic glance took in mother and daughter. 'I'll go and arrange for admittance and be back to talk to you soon.'

'Jodie will be here, monitoring you, and ring the bell any time.' Emily squeezed Rachel's shoulder and followed Linton toward the desk, but he kept going to his office. Surprised, she followed him.

'Close the door.' He threw the command over his shoulder as he slammed Sam's history down onto the desk. 'Damn it, the kid's skeletal.'

His anger and frustration buffeted Emily. She understood his sense of hopelessness that in a country where food existed in overabundance this girl had chosen to starve. 'She must have been purging herself for months.'

He sat down hard, his hand raking through his hair. 'How could she possibly think that to be that thin is beautiful? I blame this celebrity culture and obsession with perfection.'

She sat on the edge of his desk. 'That's a bit too simplistic, don't you think? I think it starts a lot closer to home.' The words sounded overly definite and loud in the small room.

Linton's gaze swung around and centred exclusively on her—his green eyes penetrating way too deeply. 'How so?'

Her heart started to pound. Hell, somehow she'd just sparked his attention. No way was she going to tell Linton about Nathan. She tried to sound detached, as if she was giving an academic and professional opinion on any medical topic and not one that related to her.

'Teenagers are vulnerable as they try and work out who they are and how they fit into the world. Take someone who feels they have little control over their life. Combine that with being unhappy at how they look and add in a thoughtless, throw-away comment by someone in the family or a friend, constant teasing at school, and that can result in anorexia or bulimia.'

'Surely one comment wouldn't do it? It would have to be a bullying-type thing.' His brow creased in confusion, as if he was having problems accepting her statement.

She twisted a strand of hair around her finger as visions of her mid to late teenage years assaulted her. 'Studies have shown one comment can do it. A person can latch onto that comment and never let it go, never really see it in perspective. Or it could be a collection of random comments, building up on top of each other.'

Suddenly sympathy radiated from his eyes. 'Did that happen to you?'

His unexpected question suddenly made her academic

musings seem personal. Personal would lead to Nathan and that sent fear spiralling through her. She didn't want to see the same pity in his eyes for herself that she'd just seen reflected for Sam.

Her head whirled, trying to come up with the best way to deflect his question. Perhaps, if she gave him a snippet of her life at fifteen, that would satisfy him and he'd stop asking questions. She lifted her chin and tossed her head, her curls bouncing into her eyes. 'At fifteen I was voted least likely to be kissed by my peers, and my dad confiscated my make-up.'

Linton stiffened, as if his hand had just brushed a hot iron, and gave a tight smile. 'That sounds like the standard behaviour of some teenage girls and the normal behaviour of an over-protective father freaking out when he realised his only daughter was growing up.' His brow furrowed. 'I think you know that.'

A niggle of guilt pulled at her gut that she'd flippantly disregarded the sympathy in his original question. But she ignored it by speaking to his shoulder and avoiding his eyes. 'Let's add on my eldest brother covering my bikini and me in a woolsack. He marched me out of the dam and back to the house, hiding me from every shearer and cowboy on the station.' She crossed her arms. 'It's these sorts of things that add up.'

He narrowed his eyes, which sparked like jade. 'I think that now as an adult you know that your brothers were protecting you from the prying eyes of older, single men. Both your examples tell me you have a loving family.'

Her heart started to hammer as he sliced through her examples. She hated it that he was so perceptive. 'But it's things like this that for some kids spark off anorexia and bulimia.' The words hung defiantly between them.

'True.' He reached out his hand and lightly touched her arm. 'But I think you've told me those two stories to avoid telling me the real story.'

Her breath seemed solidify in her lungs, refusing to move in or out as the caring caress of his hand jumbled her emotions, tugging at her resolve. Memories of Nathan—vicious and soul destroying—oozed out of the deep, dark place she'd thought she successfully contained them. Beads of sweat clung to her hairline as the recollections she'd thought she'd dealt with and accepted hammered her, delivering the same sharp sting as when they'd first been inflicted.

She stood up abruptly, needing to break the contact. Needing to distance herself from the siren call of his touch. 'There is no real story.'

'I don't believe you.' He spoke softly, but the words rained down on her like hailstones, hard and painful.

She swung round, angry that he wouldn't let the topic go. 'I am *not* anorexic.'

He raised his brows. 'But you have been?'

'No.' She flung the word at him laden with hurt. 'I have never been anorexic or bulimic, and why is this conversation suddenly all about me rather than Sam?'

'Because you're hiding your body behind baggy clothes just like that fifteen-year-old, and I want to know why.'

'I dress for comfort!' She marched toward the door, needing to leave and put an end to this conversation. Her hand reached for the handle.

'You dress to bury any signs of being a woman.'

She breathed in sharply, the accuracy of his words slicing into her like a scalpel dividing skin. *Nathan's legacy.* No one else had ever deduced that she hid her body behind shapeless clothes.

Humiliation clawed at her and she wanted to sink through the floor. But she couldn't. She summoned up righteous anger, the only thing that could save her.

How dared he talk to her like that? He had no right at all. She welcomed the surge of fury that rocked through her as it numbed the pain. She spun around, her hands on her hips. 'That is complete nonsense and I need to get back to my patient.'

He checked his watch. 'Jodie is with her and technically you're off duty. But you can leave when you tell me that what I said was incorrect.'

Resentment fizzed in her veins. 'What you said was way out of line. You're my boss and you're out of order with this.'

'I'm also your friend, Emily.'

His earnest look and tone hit her like a medicine ball to the belly. Gone was every sign of the flirting, fun-loving doctor.

He splayed his fingers, palms upward in supplication. 'I get the strongest feeling something has happened to you, only I'm not sure it happened at fifteen. But whatever it is, it's trapping you.' His head moved slightly, the blond tips of his hair shining in the light. 'I want to help.'

She'd never told anyone about her year with Nathan—not her darling father or her teasing but supportive brothers. She'd been too embarrassed, too ashamed. And they'd never asked—at least, not with words. She'd been able to ignore their looks of concern when she'd returned home from uni and as she'd thrown herself into work, life had gone on. It was as if there'd been a tacit agreement that no one spoke about her time in Dubbo.

But Linton's concerned gaze bored into her. She could withstand his teasing, she could mock his flirting behaviour, but this sincerity eroded all her resolve to keep everything to herself.

Her legs suddenly gave way and she abruptly sat down, every part of her aching that he'd seen through her. She hated it that he was the *one* person who had. Now she had nowhere to hide and the galling truth had to be told. 'I accepted a while ago it was best to hide what was offensive.'

The raw pain in her voice stabbed Linton in the chest. 'What are you talking about?'

'Me.' She kept her eyes staring down as she twisted open a paperclip, straightening the wire.

'What about you?' A thousand thoughts whizzed through his mind. What was she hiding? Was she scarred from burns? Did she have a florid birthmark?

'I… Not everyone is blessed with an attractive body.'

He shook his head in disbelief, trying to shake her words into coherence. 'You think you don't have an attractive body?'

'I *know* that I don't.' Her head snapped up, her eyes glittering with daring and defiance. 'So now you've dragged that out of me and completely mortified me, you can let the subject drop, right?'

A streak of remorse twinged but he knew he had to ignore it. He couldn't stop now—he had to get to the bottom of this. The image of creamy breasts and pert buttocks that he'd glimpsed at the Royal rolled out in his mind. 'No, sorry, I can't let the subject drop. Why on earth do you think your body is unattractive?'

A shuddering sigh resonated around the room. 'You get told something often enough, you can't ignore it.'

'Who told you?' The words came out on a growl despite his intentions to sound neutral.

She dropped her gaze and her body started to shiver.

He spoke softly this time. 'Emily?'

Her hands fisted in her lap. 'A boyfriend at uni found me lacking in many attributes.'

Anger curled in his gut at the unknown man. 'This guy sounds like a complete jerk.'

For a moment her lips curved up slightly and the Emily he knew so well almost surfaced. 'I see you've met him.'

He wanted to open her eyes to this guy. 'But he was just *one* guy with *one* opinion.'

She dropped her chin, her hair falling forward, masking her expression, but he caught a glimpse of pearly white teeth nibbling her plump bottom lip.

Heat slammed into him. Hell, what was wrong with him? He pulled his concentration back. He was supposed to be helping her, not imagining what her lips would taste like. 'Other boyfriends must have cancelled out his attitude.'

'He was the *only* guy.' The mumbled words were barely audible.

Her pain rocked through him and he worried he might have pushed her too hard. He suddenly realised she might not have told anyone about this. 'I know it seems tough right now but talking about it will help.'

A moment later she raised her head, her eyes filled with a mixture of defiance and shame. 'I guess starting at the beginning works best.' She hauled in a deep breath. 'I left home at eighteen to study nursing. I was pretty naïve and definitely inexperienced, and I met Nathan toward the end of my second year. He was the first man who had ever shown any interest in me and…' She shrugged and swallowed hard. 'I guess he swept me off my feet. I remember it all happened very fast and we suddenly went from two dates a week apart to being together most of the time.'

His radar went on full alert. 'Did he pay you a lot of attention and shower you with gifts?'

'At the start, yes. He used to text me on the hour, he took me out to dinner, bought me flowers and chocolates. Then he started buying me clothes and no one had ever done anything like that for me. At first it was intoxicating to be the centre of attention when I'd always felt overlooked by men.' She looked straight at him, surprise on her face. 'How did you know he did that? Do you have a crystal ball?'

His gut turned over, aching for her. 'No, but I've met guys like that.' *Treated the women they've left emotionally damaged.*

She jabbed the paperclip onto the edge of the desk. 'By Christmas we were a couple and I was head over heels in love. He visited the station during my summer holidays. When I returned for my final year of study he suggested I move in. He said the rent would be less and I could give up my part-time job and focus on uni. Final year is pretty full on with study and practicals and he convinced me it would be a solution to make my life easier. He even turned the third bedroom into a study for me.'

'I could see how that would be tempting,' Linton murmured encouragingly. He worried she might not want to continue.

She blew out a long breath. 'That was when things started to change. He insisted on picking me up from the hospital, driving me to uni, basically not letting me be alone. He bought me clothes, suggested what I should wear. At first it seemed special, that a man would take such an interest. But then his behaviour started to be unpredictable especially if I didn't wear what he had bought.'

A shudder vibrated through her. 'There were times when

everything was as wonderful as when we first met, but they got further apart and more times than not I didn't recognise him. Like the day he cut up the dress I'd bought to wear to a friend's twenty-first.'

Anger, raw and primitive, blasted through him so hard that had he been standing he would have been knocked off his feet. This low-life had used vicious verbal abuse to crush a young woman who should have been blossoming into womanhood and discovering her own brand of sexuality.

Somehow he managed to sound calm. 'And when he acted irrationally he always blamed you. Men like that don't love, they only want to control.'

Her grey eyes filmed over and she blinked rapidly, nodding her head 'Pretty much. It was so confusing. I wanted to be attractive for him, I wanted to make him happy—I loved him—but no matter what I did, it was wrong. I was never pretty enough, I was never appreciative enough and...'

Her head shot up, her face suddenly full of strength. 'The day I found him in our bed with another student, I left.'

He reached out and picked up her hand. 'Good for you. You're far too good for a worm like him.' But although she'd walked away from this low-life, he could tell she still had the scars.

Emily smiled a wobbly smile. 'Thanks, but I'm OK. You don't have to try and make me feel better.'

I think I do. He had to make her realise she was attractive. Had to try and undo some of the low-life's conditioning. Sure, she wasn't his type of woman but she needed to know that she had qualities that deserved to be showcased. 'What he said about you not being attractive is wrong. Don't you think that four years is long enough to hold onto false impressions?'

A thousand different emotions swirled in her eyes and marched across her face, but fear dominated. She pulled her hand out from under his.

'You're twenty-five now, Emily. It's time to come out of the shadows.'

She twisted on her chair and flung him a derisive look. 'I'll put it on my "to do" list.'

If he let her leave now, nothing would be sorted out. She'd never take the risk. He had to force her to take that step. An idea suddenly exploded in his head. Sure, it wasn't quite what he'd planned but an evening with Emily wouldn't be hard. And he knew Emily never walked away from a dare.

He pulled open his top drawer and plucked out an envelope. 'The Red Cross Desperate and Dateless Ball is on this weekend.'

Her shoulders shot back, her scrubs pulling against her breasts, and her eyes widened, indignation flashing brightly. 'I am not desperate.'

He ignored the zip of sensation that zeroed in on his groin. She had no idea how sexy she looked when she got all fired up. He forced himself to lean back, to act casually. 'You're not dateless either. I dare you to come with me in a little black dress.'

Her hand immediately fisted in her hair, her forefinger tugging at a curl, winding the purple strands around it.

He glimpsed panic before it receded, quickly replaced by a spark of defiance.

Silently, she rose to her feet and walked to the door. She turned as her hand clasped the handle. 'I'll think about it and be in touch.'

She disappeared behind the door, the only evidence that she'd been in the room was the waft of perfume she'd left behind.

He couldn't believe he'd misread her, that she wouldn't rise to his dare. The axis of his world shifted slightly as disappointment, sharp and unexpected, churned his gut.

CHAPTER SIX

'SO HOW's the new job with Linton working out?' Emily's friend and Flying Doctors nurse Kate Tremont put a cup of steaming hot Earl Grey tea down on a coaster.

Emily groaned and buried her head in her arms, leaning against Kate's large jarrah kitchen table.

'That good, huh?'

She looked up into smiling brown eyes and forced herself to sit up. 'The work part is fine.'

Kate shot her a calculating look. 'Is there actually some truth to Baden's theory, then, that you fancy Linton?'

She almost choked on her tea. What on earth had happened to her? For years she'd kept everything to herself but just lately she'd said things that opened her up to difficult questions. Her embarrassing yet strangely cathartic conversation with Linton had rolled through her head almost continuously for three days straight. Now Kate was onto her.

'Emily?' Kate's expression had changed from calculating to concerned. 'Is everything OK?'

Emily sighed. 'Do you have any chocolate-coated teddy-bear biscuits? If I have to tell you this story I'm going to need chocolate.'

Kate rose gracefully and rummaged through the pantry.

'Even better, I have Florentines from the bakery.' She quickly put them on a square white dish and placed them in front of Emily. 'Will three be enough?'

Emily grinned. 'Plenty.' Kate was a good friend and Emily had been thrilled when she'd married Baden Tremont, finding happiness after such a dark time in her life. She wished she'd known such a friend when she'd been younger, when she'd been in Dubbo.

'So?' Kate nibbled on a Florentine.

She took a deep breath. 'So, Linton asked me to the Desperate and Dateless Ball.'

Kate leaned forward. 'Excellent. And you're going?'

Emily ran her finger around the rim of the teacup. 'I told him I'd think about it but really I meant no.'

'And the reason for that would be…?'

She bit her lip and pushed on. 'Because he dared me to wear a dress.'

Kate's forehead creased in a frown. 'But isn't that the sort of thing you'd be wearing anyway?'

Panic swished through her stomach. 'This is *me* we're talking about, Kate. Jeans, jumpers and boots, the occasional voluminous dress—practical clothes.'

'And that's fine for the farm, Em, but not for a ball.' Kate folded her arms and fixed her with a penetrating look. 'What are you really worried about?'

Her fear rushed out, tumbling over the words. 'That I'll look ridiculous. I've never done anything like this before and I'm not designed for elegance, I'm—'

'Nonsense.' Kate's hand hit the table with a loud slap. 'We just need to find you the right dress to show off what you've got.'

I don't have anything. Part of her wanted to believe Kate

but most of her didn't. 'Oh, right, and Warragurra's one dress shop is going to have that dress? I don't think so, which is why I have to say no.' She glared at Kate. 'I will *not* make a fool of myself.'

'I won't let you do that.' The quiet words were delivered with feeling.

And she knew Kate spoke the truth. Tall and graceful, she had an innate sense of style and Emily knew she'd be in good hands. For a moment the sincerity in Kate's voice reassured her, but then the terrors instilled by Nathan rose again. *Cover yourself up, you don't want to put people off their dinner.*

Linton's warm voice vibrated inside her. *Men like that don't love, they only want to control.* She tried to hold onto that thought, pushing Nathan's legacy out.

'Do you want to snag Linton's attention and have him see you in a new way, not as Unit Manager, not as a friend, but as a woman?'

Her stomach churned, driving acid to the back of her throat. 'I… Well, part of me does.' *But what if I'm a disappointment?* That fear had plagued her since high school and more so since she'd left Nathan. It had held her back from ever thinking about another relationship.

Kate smiled. 'Then the solution is easy. We're going to Sydney and we're buying a dress.'

The sensation of being on a runaway train exploded inside her and she scrambled for some control. 'I can't just go to Sydney.' Her voice rose a little higher on each word.

'Sure you can. We've both got days off. I'll book the flights now. Sasha can come with us, she'll love an excuse to shop in Sydney.' Kate clapped in delight. 'It will be a girls' day out, and as Linton dared you to wear the dress, he can pay.'

Kate handed Emily the phone. 'Ring him now and tell him you're going to the ball.'

Kate's eyes glinted with determination and Emily knew right there and then that there was no way out. She'd never realised Cinderella's fairy godmother must have doubled as a bulldozer.

Emily stood shaking in black, lacy underwear, sheer stockings and high heels, staring at the little black dress she'd gone to Sydney to buy. She wished Kate and Sasha Tremont were standing with her right now. Kate had insisted this was *the* dress. Sasha, at twelve, had wanted her to buy the one with the large pink bow.

When she'd baulked at the dress Kate had run roughshod over every excuse and had declared this to be the dress to impress. A traitorous part of her *so* wanted to impress that she'd given in entirely and gone with Kate's choice.

Linton's comments about Nathan had bolstered her confidence into a shaky self-belief. Perhaps Nathan had been wrong. His words still played in her head but the volume was low and the sound quality buzzed with static.

But now with Linton about to arrive, panic clawed at her. What had she let Kate and Linton talk her into? She stared at her reflection, not recognising the person staring back. Her carefully styled hair curved around her face and her make-up looked straight out of a magazine, courtesy of the beautician who had written down detailed instructions for her.

The dress was the last piece of the puzzle.

Putting it on was technically the easy part. Facing her father and her brothers, facing Linton, had her stomach doing continuous somersaults.

Her fingers fumbled as she fastened her mother's pearls

around her neck. It didn't matter that she was twenty-five, didn't matter that she was an experienced nurse—she couldn't walk out there. What if she got the same reaction that Nathan had given her?

Her legs wobbled like jelly.

I dare you to come with me. Linton's teasing words echoed in her head again, just like they'd been doing for the last week.

'Hey, sis, there's a car coming up the drive.' Mark rapped on her door.

Her heart pounded so hard that she glanced down, expecting to see it moving against her chest. She couldn't do this. She couldn't go out there.

Her mouth dried at the alternative. Her father and brothers would demand to know why. Telling Linton about Nathan had been bad enough. She had to go out in this dress.

'Em, you OK?' Mark's muffled voice came under the door.

'Yes, fine.' She forced the words out against her constricted throat and reached for the dress.

With shaking fingers she slipped it over her head.

Linton bounded up the farmhouse steps, pulling on his dinner jacket at the same time. He'd been late getting away and he really regretted it. He had a niggling feeling that being ten minutes late could be enough to make Emily bail on him.

He'd been pleasantly surprised when he'd taken her phone call saying she'd come to the ball. And he'd laughed when she'd matched his dare by telling him he was paying for the dress. Parting with a few hundred dollars for a dress was a small price to pay if he could help her redefine herself.

He knew she'd bought a dress because he'd received a phone call from the exclusive Sydney Double Bay boutique.

But would she wear it? All day he'd half expected a text saying she wasn't coming.

The front door opened as he approached and a solid, middle-aged man extended his hand in greeting. 'Jim Tippett.'

'Linton Gregory.' He returned the strong handshake.

'Come in.' Jim stretched out his arm. 'Have you met Mark, Stuart and Eric, three of Emily's brothers?'

The men stood in a semi-circle, their wide-legged stance declaring this was their territory. They all nodded in silent greeting and shook his hand. Time rolled back to what he imagined life would have been like forty years ago. Linton had the distinct impression he was being assessed for suitability to date their sister.

'We thought you might have missed the turn-off in the dark.' Jim raised one reddish brow.

Linton read the code encrypted in the statement. *You're late—never make a woman wait.*

'Dad, ten minutes late means Linton is actually on time.'

All the men spun around toward the slightly husky voice. Emily stood at the edge of the room, clutching a tiny beaded evening bag, her eyes silver and hesitant.

Linton's breath stalled in his chest as a wave of heat thudded through him.

Her purple hair had vanished. Now Titian curls hovered around her cheeks, softening her face the way natural hair colour did. But her hair was only one change.

A fitted black lace bodice clung to more curves than he could ever have imagined existed under the sack-like clothes she normally wore. Bare, creamy shoulders teased the eye but the bombshell was the drop pearl necklace that nestled in the dip between her breasts, hinting at the generous softness that hid behind the dress.

A froth of tulle fell from a tiny waist, the layers finishing just below her knees. Shapely legs narrowed down to small feet, which were clad in strappy sandals, giving her extra height and an aura of elegance that he'd never associated with Emily.

The transformation stole all coherent thought.

'Who are you and what have you done with my sister?' Mark broke the stunned silence with a cheeky grin.

Jim beamed proudly. 'Don't listen to your brother. You're all grown up and you look as beautiful as your mother did the first time I met her.'

'Really?' Emily's tongue darted out and flicked at her glossy bottom lip.

Silver lights flashed danced in Linton's head as his blood pounded south.

'Of course you do.' Jim kissed her on the cheek and spoke again, this time his voice full of emotion. 'I probably should have told you that more often.' He turned abruptly to Linton, a chuckle on his lips. 'You all right, son?'

The words penetrated the inert haze of Linton's brain and he realised he'd been standing silently, staring like a fourteen-year-old. He propelled himself into action. He presented his arm to Emily. 'Your chariot awaits, Ms Tippett.'

She grinned and slid her arm through his, the slight weight of her arm fitting against his as if it had been made to sit there. As if it belonged there.

He immediately shrugged the feeling away.

Tonight was just an extension of work and Emily was his partner just for the evening.

The Royal's ballroom was almost unrecognisable. Red velvet fabric draped the furniture and red chiffon covered the walls, the filmy material softening the large area. Pearly red helium balloons filled the enormous ceiling space, their silver curling ribbon tails sparkling in the faux candlelight. Even the huge cherub ice statue was backlit by a red spotlight.

Linton took a break and drank some non-alcoholic fruit punch, which was, of course, red. He'd danced with almost every attractive woman at the ball, but he'd battled to get a passing glance from his partner for the evening. Far too many attentive cowboys were dancing with her. Ben McCreedy had held her very tightly with his good arm and Daniel and Jason had been acting like lust-struck puppies all night.

Oh, right, and you haven't?

The image of Emily standing hesitantly in her father's lounge room with the naked need of approval hovering in her eyes and a body that could have modelled swimwear had branded itself deeply in his mind. And it kept playing over and over and over.

He tugged at his collar, suddenly finding the bow-tie constricting. Funny, in Sydney he wore black tie once a fortnight and the tie had never bothered him. Usually he enjoyed these gala events where everyone dressed up and raised money for a worthwhile cause. Even though he hadn't been short of company tonight, his usual sense of freedom that came from numerous dance partners and plenty of conversation seemed to have deserted him. He rolled his shoulders back. It was like he had an unscratchable itch, making him prickly and out of sorts.

He scanned the room again for Emily, but without her signature bright hair she was harder to spot. He batted away some red helium balloons, which had started to hover lower, their tails hitting him across his face. He finally found her dancing with Baden.

He moved in, tapping the Flying Doctor's shoulder. 'Shouldn't you be dancing with your wife?'

Baden laughed. 'Well, I suppose as you paid for the dress, you should get at least one dance.' He spun Emily out of his arms and into Linton's.

Sparkling eyes appraised him with a familiar mocking glint as they swayed to a rock and roll tune. 'You've been busy tonight.'

A sliver of umbrage caught him. 'Hey, I could say the same thing about you.'

She laughed, the tone flirting and wicked. 'I was just keeping busy until there was a break in the queue of women wanting to dance with you. After all, I wouldn't want your reputation as Warragurra's resident playboy to be ruined by you dancing with me twice.' She spun out in a twirl.

He brought her back, his arm firm against her waist, her breasts brushing his chest. A tingle of sensation burned through him. 'My reputation will survive me dancing more than two dances.' *But will you?*

The voice in his head was forgotten as he caught a flash of surprise in her eyes. Hell, did she really think he hadn't wanted to dance with her? He'd tried many times to, but the line for her had been as constant as his own. Surely after the success of tonight she no longer thought she was unattractive?

He dropped his head close to hers, his chin almost resting on her shoulder, and whispered, 'And who knew you had red hair?'

She twirled out laughing and came back facing him, wrinkling her decidedly cute nose. 'Yeah, well, don't even think about going there. That was another torment in my life. Red hair *and* freckles.'

The music slowed and he felt her back stiffen as if she was

about to walk away. He tightened his arm and drew her fractionally closer. Even in heels her head would fit neatly under his chin if she wasn't holding her neck rigid with her chin pointed upward in that, oh, so familiar position.

Her perfume circled him, its sensual spice now so in tune with its wearer. 'You look completely sensational tonight.'

She stared up at him, her eyes like platinum pools. 'Thank you. And thanks for the dress.'

'My pleasure.' It was a standard response—one he used many times a day when he received thanks. Except the wave of uncomplicated happiness that rolled through him, followed by a trailing alien sense of wellbeing, was far from standard. Nothing about this night was standard.

Emily's brain struggled to keep up with everything that had happened from the moment she had stepped into the Royal's ballroom. It was like her world had been turned upside down and she was dizzy, trying to adjust to all the changes. Granted, she'd avoided social functions like this but even so she'd been stunned by the response she'd received from both men and women.

The men had wanted to dance with her. The woman had wanted to gossip about the dress. Kate had been right—the dress had impressed.

And Linton's gaze had been fixed on her for most of the evening. She wasn't a disappointment. A thrill of joy raced through her as she gave herself up to savouring the sensation of being held firmly in his arms.

He danced her out toward the veranda, away from the crowd, the music and the noise of two hundred people talking. The cool evening air washed over them as they twirled through the French doors.

He spun her around and she came to rest against him, her back against his chest, feeling his warmth radiating into her, the pressure of his arm across her waist. Feeling protected. Safe.

With sudden clarity she realised she'd felt that way with him ever since she'd told him about Nathan. He'd accepted her, had not judged her.

She turned in his arms and looked up into his smiling face, his scent of soap and citrus aftershave tingling in her nostrils as she breathed in. 'I almost didn't come tonight.'

He nodded, complete understanding radiating from his eyes. 'I know what a huge step this has been for you. Keep telling yourself this—Nathan is pond scum. Don't let his warped view taint you.' He tucked a stray curl behind her ear.

The light touch sent ribbons of wonder through her, both his actions and words bolstering her fledgling confidence. She realised that, despite her misgivings, telling Linton her story had actually helped her. Trusting him had been the best thing she'd done in four long years.

He was right—she had been hiding. She'd been holding back, holding back from life and keeping her attraction to him a secret. Scared of being a disappointment. But perhaps she didn't have to hide any more.

She gazed up at him, glorying in the look of undisguised desire in his eyes. At that very moment she knew he wanted to kiss her.

And she had no objection at all.

Linton gazed down into her upturned face. Her cheeks glowed pink, luminous grey eyes sparkled with silver, and slightly parted red lips shone like a beacon, daring him to taste.

He never could walk away from a dare.

She moved her palm flat against his chest, her heat scorching him.

Silver lights fired in his head as sensation exploded inside him, knocking hard against his resolve that this was all part of work.

He lowered his lips to hers, tasting strawberries, champagne and fresh air. Feeling lush softness that yielded to his touch and yet returned a pressure that gently demanded more.

Her mouth slowly opened under his, the action full of tentative reserve but overlaid with an invitation to come in and explore. The innocence of the action, so amazingly sexy, drove out all rational thought.

The noise, the music, all sounds of the evening faded as he slid his right hand up along her back, gently cradling her neck and firmly holding her mouth to his.

Blood pounded loudly in his ears as every part of him urged him to deepen the kiss, to taste the ambrosia of her mouth.

But an unfamiliar yet delicious lassitude stole through him, unexpectedly powerful, slowing him down and making him savour this moment.

Lips explored lips. Small nibbling bites, long caressing licks—a millimetre-by-millimetre journey, leaving no space untouched.

Her mouth traversed his lips, each stroke sparking a trail of glorious sensation, each trail spiralling down deeper than the last until all trails merged, coursing through him and energising him like no other kiss ever had.

As if reading his mind, she suddenly leaned in.

Now more than lips touched. Her breasts flattened against his chest as her arms slid around his neck. A soft sigh—half sated, half demanding—tumbled from her mouth as her tongue flicked across his teeth, seeking entry, all hesitancy gone.

A wall of fiery heat exploded in his chest, his need for her burning quickly through the restraint he'd happily welcomed a few minutes ago. His left hand slid from her hip to her bottom, clamping her against him, moulding her to him from ankle to lips, until no space between them existed.

She tilted her head back and he plundered her mouth. Sweetness meshed with experience, heat danced with fire, need collided with need, the explosion unleashing a carefully contained yearning that wound through him, softening years of resolve.

An edge of panic moved into place. *Spend the night but not a lifetime. Don't let a woman trap you.* His father's voice boomed in his head.

'Supper's served,' a voice called out into the dark of the veranda.

He felt a shudder against him and then cool night air caressed his lips and quickly stole down his body. Emily stepped back. 'Great. I'm starving.'

She stood in the shadows, her expression unreadable. An irrational sense of loss lingered, tinged with aggravation that her desire for food sounded stronger than her desire for him.

She caught his hand in a friendly gesture. 'Come on, or the queue for the chocolate fountain will be a mile long.'

She tugged him back into the ballroom, the bright lights and noise making him blink. Nothing looked quite the same. He shook his head. What the hell was wrong with him?

He'd kissed a hundred women at dances over the years. Tall women, stylish women, socialites, divas, blondes and brunettes—all his type of women. All of whom he'd kissed and forgotten. Kissed and moved on.

This was *no* different. If anything, it should be more easily forgotten. Emily, at barely five feet three and free of urban sophistication, was not his type of woman at all.

They reached the chocolate fountain, and she turned, smiling up at him, her lips red, soft and enticing.

His mouth tingled and the need to kiss her again surged inside him like an addiction, jolting him down to his toes.

Emily sat cuddled up next to Linton on the outdoor rattan couch, a soft blanket draped around them warding off the chill of the early morning air. Dappled moonlight lit the usually dark corner of the veranda and the crickets' song serenaded them. Two black and white dogs lay curled up close by, dreaming of chasing sheep.

It had been the most amazing evening of her life and the euphoria of the ball still bubbled in her veins. From the moment Linton had cut in on her dance with Baden, he hadn't left her side.

And he'd kissed her—gloriously, deliciously and wonderfully—until her body had been molten and her brain had been unable to assemble a single coherent thought.

Linton's mouth nibbled her ear. Need, hot and raw, speared down deep inside her. She'd imagined his kisses but no amount of daydreaming had prepared her for the reality.

He trailed kisses down her neck and across her collarbone, lingering in the hollow at her throat, his tongue doing wicked things, stirring up such a strong response she risked losing complete control.

It's happening too fast. Somewhere from deep inside her a warning voice sounded faintly. She placed her hands on his solid chest, gaining some space between their bodies. But her palms revelled in the touch of his smooth, hot skin and she gave in to the tempting sensation to run her fingers down his ribs, tickling him under the last one.

His head shot up, laughter on his lips and danger in his eyes. 'Hey. You want to play a different game, do you?'

He reached under the blanket but his hands got tangled in the layers of tulle. 'What on earth...?'

She started to giggle and put her fingers to her lips. 'Shh, we don't want to wake anyone up.'

'Yeah, your brothers might turn up with a shotgun.' He pulled her close and whispered. 'Your family is very protective of you.'

She laid her head on his shoulder, enjoying the sensation of the fine soft cotton of his shirt under her cheek. 'No, they're not.'

'Yes, they are. Your dad was giving me "take care of my little girl" signals from the moment I arrived and your brothers gave me *the look*.'

She raised her head and stared into green eyes that reflected the moon. 'What look?'

'The look that said, "Put one foot wrong and we'll beat you to a pulp".'

She sighed and laid her head back down. 'Sorry about that.'

His fingers tightened at her waist. 'No need to be sorry. You're really lucky.'

'Lucky?' Her finger fiddled with one of his shirt buttons. 'How is it lucky to have five men organising your life for you?'

His hand gently captured hers and held it against his chest. 'At least they care. I get the impression your brothers would walk through fire for you.'

She shrugged. 'I suppose, but that's what family is all

Play The *Lucky Hearts* Game

and get...
FREE BOOKS & a FREE GIFT... YOURS to KEEP!

Yes! I have scratched off the silver card. Please send me my **FREE BOOKS** and **FREE MYSTERY GIFT**. I understand that I am under no obligation to purchase any books as explained on the back of this card. I am over 18 years of age.

Scratch Here!
then look below to see
what you can claim...

M8II8

Mrs/Miss/Ms/Mr _____ Initials _____

BLOCK CAPITALS PLEASE

Surname _____

Address _____

_____

Postcode _____

Twenty-one gets you
4 FREE BOOKS and a
MYSTERY GIFT!

Twenty gets you
1 FREE BOOK and a
MYSTERY GIFT!

Nineteen gets you
1 FREE BOOK!

TRY AGAIN!

THE MILLS & BOON® BOOK CLUB™
FREE BOOK OFFER
FREEPOST CN81
CROYDON
CR9 3WZ

NO STAMP
NECESSARY
IF POSTED IN
THE U.K. OR N.I.

about. For better or worse, they're there for you even if half
the time they're frustrating the life out of you.' She wriggled
against him as she brought her feet up under the blanket.
'How do you get along with your brothers?'

He stiffened. 'I don't have any brothers.'

His tension and the tone of voice made her study him
closely. Shadows moved in his eyes but that could have been
the moonlight. 'Sisters? I bet you're a protective big brother,
just like Mark.'

'Nope, no sisters.' The words shot out brisk and abrupt.
'I'm an only child.'

Sadness skittered through her at the bald statement. Her
brothers might sometimes drive her crazy but she had plenty
of fond memories of riotous games of Monopoly, stories
around the campfire when they had been out mustering and
even fun times doing mundane chores like drying the dishes
at night. She had a strong urge to make him feel better about
this. 'At least you didn't have to fight for your parents' attention—that has to be a bonus.'

He grimaced. 'For many years they were too busy fighting
each other. They divorced when I was twelve.'

The chill in his words made her shiver. 'Oh, that would
have been tough. Was not being able to have more children
part of the problem?'

'No, having me *was* the problem.' Acrimony filled his
voice. 'I was the accident, the reason for their ill-conceived
marriage. At eighteen neither of them was ready for that sort
of responsibility.' He sighed. 'Their divorce was inevitable
from day one.'

Pain, raw and jagged, slugged her. 'At least they tried to
make it work.'

'I suppose.' He sounded unconvinced. 'All I remember is

the bitterness and rancour. It was a relief when they divorced. They still hated each other but at least home was quiet and free of arguments.' He ran his free hand across the back of his neck in a now familiar reaction to stress.

She'd lost her mother but her father and her brothers had given her a lot of happy times. Life on the station had been calm and supportive. 'Did either of your parents remarry?'

He cleared his throat. 'My mother married her university professor a year after the divorce. Cliff's OK. He tried too hard to be the "responsible" parent. Neither he nor Mum approved of Dad's post-divorce lifestyle.'

Intrigue drove her questions. 'Did you see much of your father, growing up?'

He nodded. 'I spent the school holidays with him. His business took off a year after the divorce and he became quite wealthy. Going to Dad's was like entering a different world, a world without boundaries or rules. I loved it. I got to meet all sorts of people, although the summer Dad dated a series of swimwear models is the year I remember most vividly.'

He laughed. 'I learned *very* quickly to only tell each parent the bare minium about my time in the ex-spouse's household. Mum and Cliff would have had a court order preventing me from going to Dad's if they'd known less than half of what went on.'

'What sort of things?'

'If I tell you, I might have to kill you.' His aura of melancholy evaporated and he gently kissed her fingertips, his mouth slowly moving along her hand and up her arm. 'You taste absolutely wonderful. I could kiss you all night.'

She hugged his words close. This was what she'd dreamed of on all those long and lonely nights.

Go slowly, remember Nathan. The faint voice gained

volume but Linton's mouth reached her jaw, sapping her concentration.

Each touch of his lips fired her blood, each touch stoking her response, tightening her breasts into tingling swirls and fanning out liquid heat between her legs, urging her to lie back and savour the ministrations of the man she adored.

He groaned and slid his hand along her leg, avoiding the entanglement of the tulle. 'Seeing you tonight was like finding hidden treasure.'

His thick voice couldn't hide his desire. He kissed the edge of her mouth and her body moved toward his, needing his touch like it needed air.

You're not treasure, you're not a possession. The uncooperative part of her brain stayed focused and forced her to stay on track with the conversation. 'Did your dad remarry?'

Linton paused, his lips resting warm and firm on her jaw. 'Hell, no.'

His emphatic response drove a stake of unease into her.

He trailed butterfly kisses across her cheek but she refused to be distracted. 'Why "Hell, no"?'

His hand caressed her hair. 'He's having far too much fun to ever tie himself down to marriage.'

Just like his son. The words exploded in her head with the deafening boom of a bomb.

The playboy doctor.

The man who never dated a woman more than once. The man who in the past year had never dated her, never even looked twice at her.

Seeing you tonight was like finding hidden treasure.

She drew in a ragged breath. He'd noticed her tonight when she'd met his dare and dressed up especially for him. Had his dare been more about what he wanted than about helping her?

A bitter taste filled her mouth. Oh, what had she done?

Like a balloon snagging on a thorn, her wonderful evening popped and her euphoria cascaded over her, clawing at her mouth and nose, suffocating her. Why did she make such appalling choices with men? She'd been so dumb. So stupid.

She'd trusted Linton. She'd thought he understood her. But he didn't because right now he only had eyes for a body that caused her grief, whether it was hidden or on display.

Nathan had forced her to cover up. Linton had pushed her to uncover. Both had pushed for what *they'd* wanted.

And she'd let herself be pushed. The realisation rocked her. Neither of them really knew her or what made her tick.

Do you know yourself?

The hard truth sent her blood plummeting to her feet. She'd always been so scared she'd disappoint that she recreated herself for those around her. Just like she'd done with Nathan. Just like she'd done tonight.

Linton had accused her of hiding and she still was—it was just that the costume was different.

How could she expect anyone to consider what she wanted when she didn't know herself? The thought acted like a steel support running the length of her spine. She needed to take stock and work out what she wanted, who she really was.

But in the confusing mess of this realisation, there was one thing she knew for sure. Linton didn't really want *her*. He didn't care what was inside the package; he just wanted to play with the sparkly gift-wrap. He was bewitched by her body—a fake façade.

Well, she didn't want to be plundered treasure and she refused to be fool's gold.

She deserved better than that.

CHAPTER SEVEN

LINTON bounced into A and E remarkably full of energy despite little sleep. At two a.m. Emily had reminded him that she had to be on duty at eight so he'd reluctantly relinquished her from his arms and headed home.

He should have slept well.

Instead, he'd tossed and turned and he couldn't blame stifling summer heat or concern about a patient. He really should have slept well. But every time he'd closed his eyes, his arms had ached for a petite redhead with audacious, sparkling eyes.

So he'd given up trying to sleep. Not that he'd admit that to anyone, especially Baden Tremont. For some inexplicable reason his brain had kept returning to Emily's mouth and every single kiss.

And there'd been many.

He hadn't kissed like that since… Come to think of it, he'd never kissed like that before. Usually the kiss, although very enjoyable, was a perfunctory preamble to further exploration. But Emily's lush mouth had captivated him from the first moment and he couldn't get enough of it.

The whole evening had felt surreal. Emily had a siren's body made for lusty tumbles and her mouth had intoxicated him with her brand of kisses—a mixture of innocence and growing confidence. From the first touch he'd been lost in the wonder of her mouth and the craziest thing had happened. He'd been possessed by this overwhelming need to protect her and it had controlled him all night.

Even now, six hours later, he couldn't quite fathom how that had happened. So, instead of suggesting she come and have coffee at his place, he'd taken her back to her father's house and spent an hour necking on the porch, stealing kisses like a seventeen-year-old. Hell, he'd been far more restrained than a seventeen-year-old. He'd only got as far as running his hand up the back of her leg before she'd reminded him of the time.

He couldn't wait to go on from where he'd left off and he had the perfect plan. Emily would be off at two and they could picnic at Ledger's Gorge. It might even be warm enough to swim. An image of what Emily would look like in a bikini thudded through him and sweat broke out on his top lip.

Emily's not like Penelope. The thought quickly skated across his brain, fading away as he caught sight of Jodie.

'Morning, Linton.' Jodie looked up from her end-of-shift reports, the only nurse at the desk.

'Morning.' He found himself glancing around, looking for Emily, but she was nowhere to be seen. Disappointment rammed him hard. He pulled on his white coat and glanced at the clear board. 'Busy night and you've moved everyone on?'

Jodie shook her head. 'Really quiet. I think Patti and I had a much quieter time than you did.' She grinned. 'I hear the ball was fabulous.'

His lips curved up in a broad smile. It was probably a ridiculously silly grin but he couldn't help himself. 'So Emily's given you all the lowdown on the frocks and the suits, all the girly gossip?'

'No, she's not in yet.'

Startled, he glanced at his watch while Jodie continued talking. It wasn't like Emily to be late.

'Jason and Daniel dropped in at three a.m. with coffee and some food they'd sneaked out for us. They regaled us with stories.' Jodie swept some paper plates and disposable coffee-cups off the desk and into the bin as the doors opened.

'Jodie, please grab an ophthalmology kit from the supply room.' Emily walked in, issuing orders and supporting Daryl Heath, the police sergeant. She glanced at Linton, her grey eyes flicking over him, their expression neutral. 'It's good that you're here, Linton, because Daryl needs a doctor.'

She walked past with their patient toward the resus room, her shimmering cobalt blue hair vivid against her regulation-issue green scrubs.

Linton stood bolted to the floor, staring after them and blinking rapidly. *Bright blue hair.* Subconsciously he'd known Emily wouldn't be in a figure-hugging ballgown at work but he hadn't expected this, not after last night. What was going on? He quickly picked up his stethoscope and followed them.

Emily had placed an eye patch over Daryl's eye and was taking his blood pressure, the stethoscope in her ears conveniently preventing any conversation. Not that he could talk to her about anything other than their patient, and from the defiant tilt of her chin she knew that.

'What brings you in to see us this early Sunday morning, Daryl? I thought after last night you'd be having a sleep-in.' Linton shook the well-respected officer's hand.

'The Red Cross know how to throw a good bash, don't

they? But I must have done something to my eye because this morning it's throbbing so hard it feels like it might pop out of my head.' His hand formed a fist by his side, as if he was trying hard not to rub his eye to soothe it.

'It got so sore so fast I thought I better come in and see you.' He glanced around at all the equipment and shivered. 'I don't think I'm so sick that I need to be in here, though.'

Linton grinned. 'We need a room that we can darken so we can examine your eye properly. That's why Emily sat you in this chair, rather than getting you up on the trolley.' He leaned forward and lifted the eye patch.

The area around the eye was puffy and the eyelid was swollen. Red lines criss-crossed the sclera, which should have been white. The whole area looked angry and sore.

He turned on his ophthalmoscope and peered through the small aperture, the tiny globe providing the light to examine the eye. The conjunctiva, the thin, transparent covering of the eye, was also swollen and red.

'He's got a slight temp of 37.8 Celsius.' Emily read out the digital display the moment the ear thermometer beeped, her voice professional and clipped. 'Other observations are within normal limits.'

He didn't miss the fact she'd given the observations information when he couldn't look at her, or that every action of hers seemed stiff and starchy this morning. Last night's Emily seemed a figment of his imagination in more ways than one.

Daryl's pupil, which should have contracted to a small black disc in reaction to the bright light, reacted sluggishly. A red flag waved in Linton's brain. He switched off the ophthalmoscope and put a new eye patch over the good eye. 'What line can you read on the chart?'

'Your glasses were so dirty that everything would have

been out of focus,' Emily gently chided as she passed Daryl his glasses, which she'd cleaned with a soft cloth.

The patient leaned forward, squinting. 'Hell, can I start at the third line?'

'Sure, start where you can.' Linton caught a sudden flash of blue out of the corner of his eye. He turned to see Emily nibbling her bottom lip in concern. The memory of the touch of those lips on his mouth blasted through him in a wave of heat.

Daryl's recitation of the third line of the chart grounded him and he fished his pen out of his top pocket. 'I want you to follow the pen for me with your eye, not your head.' He held it in the midline of vision and slowly moved it to the left.

Daryl's eye started to move but he suddenly raised his palm to cover it. 'Fair go, Doc, that doesn't tickle.'

Emily silently handed him a bottle of fluorescein, an eye dye to expose a damaged cornea.

'Thanks.' He smiled at her and caught a shadow darken her eyes to a cloudy grey before she turned to pick up a bottle of solution.

'Daryl, I need you to tip your head back and as soon as I've put these drops in I need you to blink to distribute the dye.' He carefully administered the single drop to the lower conjunctival sac.

Daryl blinked rapidly.

Emily leaned forward and tucked a towel around Daryl's shoulders. 'Now I'm going to squirt some saline in your eye to remove the excess dye and see if something has gone into your eye and caused some damage.'

'It's a bit of a rigmarole, isn't it?' Daryl obediently tilted his head back and held the edge of the towel to his face.

'Now I need you to rest your chin here.' Emily pointed

to the chin rest on the slit lamp and helped their patient get into position.

Linton explained the procedure. 'I'm looking for blue dye. There's quite a bit of it about today and not all of it is in your eye.'

Emily smiled sweetly and ignored him. 'Daryl, what Linton is trying to say is that if you've done any damage to your cornea the dye will stick to it and show up as blue.'

Linton leaned into the slit lamp, putting his eye against the aperture and muttered, 'Pretty much like the damage Emily's done to her hair.'

He heard her sharp intake of breath. Good. At least he'd got a reaction rather than the cool, distant nurse persona.

'All set.' Linton leaned into position, his eye up against the aperture.

Emily flicked off the lights, plunging the room into darkness.

Using the blue light filter, Linton examined the eye but he couldn't detect any blue dye at all. He sighed. Seeing the dye would have been a nice easy diagnosis but that wasn't going to happen. Meanwhile, he had a patient whose vision was less than normal, had a pain on eye movement and a sluggish pupil response. It wasn't looking good. 'You can turn the lights on again, please, Emily.'

He moved the slit lamp out of the way and sat again, facing Daryl. 'The good news is the cornea isn't damaged.'

'And the bad news?' the sergeant responded instantly. He obviously knew the 'good news, bad news' scenario, as he had probably used it himself in his job.

'I'm working on a diagnosis.' Linton's brain whirred, delving into stored knowledge. 'Have you had a cold lately?' He gently tapped Daryl's face around the sinuses. 'Any pain here over the last week?'

'Yeah, I had a few headaches last week. I was taking horse-radish and garlic tablets and Nance had me on eucalyptus inhalations. I even tried the cold tablets—you know the ones that dry you up.'

The blurred edges around the symptoms suddenly sharpened into crystal-clear focus. 'I'm pretty sure you've got orbital cellulitis.'

'What's that?' Daryl's brow creased at the unfamiliar words.

Linton translated. 'The infection from your sinuses has gone across to your eye.'

'Is it serious?'

'It is if we don't treat it. Orbital cellulitis is one of those things that comes under the heading of "Act fast". I'm afraid you're going to be spending a few days with us while we put in a drip and give you IV antibiotics. The visiting ophthalmologist is due in next week so he can see you then, but meanwhile I'll talk to him by teleconference to confirm my diagnosis.'

Emily patted Daryl's arm reassuringly. 'You did the right thing coming in and in a few days you'll be feeling a lot better.' She slid a tourniquet up his arm, tightening it against his biceps. She glanced at Linton. 'If you write up the order now, I'll set up the antibiotics and give him some analgesia.'

A spark of irritation skated through Linton as he clicked his pen and picked up the chart. What she really meant was, *I've got it covered, you can leave.* Well, he wasn't leaving until he was good and ready. And not until he'd talked to Emily on her own.

'Are you allergic to penicillin, Daryl?'

'Nope, had it before with no side effects.'

'Great.' He put the authorised drug chart on the trolley, giving Emily a long questioning look.

She busied herself inserting the IV.

Linton swallowed a sigh. 'Daryl, I'll ring Nancy and tell her to pack you a bag and then you can give her a ring when you get settled up on the ward.'

The sergeant nodded. 'Thanks, Doc. She'll get a surprise that I'm here. She was still asleep so I sneaked out when the pain got a bit much.'

'You probably shouldn't have driven with your eye like that,' he gently rebuked the experienced police officer.

A chastened expression merged with one of affection. 'I didn't want to wake her.'

Linton marvelled at the care and consideration Daryl had shown his wife, despite the pain he must have been in. He couldn't remember a single moment when his parents had shown any sort of thoughtfulness toward each other.

'Emily, give the first dose of antibiotics now, and then Daryl can go upstairs. Get Jason to transfer him when you're ready.'

She nodded her understanding. 'Yes, Doctor. You can make your call now. Daryl and I are just fine.'

In other words, *you can leave now*. Well, two could play at that game. 'Catch you later, Daryl.'

He strode out of the room, his steps purposeful and determined. Emily might think he was leaving but he had another plan entirely.

He made the call to the ophthalmologist in Sydney, confirming his diagnosis and treatment plan, and then he walked out the front door of the hospital.

Town was still very quiet. The only people joining the keen cyclists were parents of young children who were out walking slowly and closely examining every insect, flower, tree and cat they came across. How did they do it? It would take an hour to walk the length of the street. Being a parent wasn't something he spent any time thinking about. His parents' botched job hadn't made him want to have a long-term relationship, let alone be a parent.

He passed a couple who stood holding hands while they indulgently watched their toddler pointing excitedly to a butterfly. Their exchanged glances, so full of devotion and love, punched him unexpectedly in the gut, making him stagger.

He needed coffee.

He went to the bakery, which had just installed a brand-new coffee-machine imported from Italy, along with an Italian cousin, who at twenty-five had the local girls flocking to watch him *barista* with flair and drool over his accent. Cosmopolitan Milan had collided with Warragurra.

'*Buon giorno.*'

'Morning, Paolo. I need a decaf latte—'

'No, *Dottore*, it is Sunday morning. You do not want decaf.'

Linton laughed. 'Very true, Paolo, I want an espresso but Emily usually has a decaf, doesn't she?'

'Not on a Sunday. On Sunday mornings I only serve strong coffee, and especially this Sunday after the ball. You take one sugar for Emily. I see she has an accident with her hair. She needs sugar.'

'She needs something,' Linton muttered to himself as he grabbed the Sunday paper and some freshly baked Danish pastries. With the paper under his arm, his coffee-cups stacked and his free hand clutching the brown bag of pastries, he headed back to A and E.

By the time he arrived, Daryl had been transferred to the ward, Jodie had gone home, the board was empty again and he found Emily furiously cleaning the pan room, her blue hair almost neon under the fluorescent light.

He deliberately stood in the doorway. 'I've got coffee.'

She stopped and turned, her smile losing a tug of war with the rest of the muscles in her face. 'Thanks. I'll be there in a minute.'

'I meant *real* coffee, from Tatti's. Paolo's made it for you just how you like it. Come now or it will be cold and he'll never forgive you.' He stayed still until she peeled off her gloves with a resigned shrug.

He moved back to allow her though the door, unable to stop himself from breathing deeply, wanting to catch a waft of the perfume that he now associated so strongly with Emily. He followed her back to the desk, admiring the way her scrubs moved across her bottom as her hips swayed.

You're pathetic.

Shut up.

The war of words spun in his head but he felt strangely disconnected from them, his attention fully on Emily. He popped the top off her coffee and passed it to her. There was no point beating about the bush. 'What have you done to your hair?'

Her cup stalled at her cherry-red lips. 'I told you, I never liked red hair.' She put the cup down and rummaged through the filing cabinet. 'What have you done with the roster?'

'What have you done with the woman I danced with last night?' The question he'd wanted to ask since she'd walked into work this morning shot out of his mouth uncensored.

Her busy hands froze on top of the files, her shoulders rigid. She turned around and faced him, her face working hard to be free of expression, but her flashing eyes gave everything away.

'Cinderella's gone and now you're left with the real me. Last night wasn't real, Linton. Last night was a bit of fairy dust and make-believe. Granted, it lasted two hours past midnight but then life went back to normal.' She pointed to her head and plucked at the V of her top. 'This *is* me.'

The confusion he'd battled with since her arrival won out. 'No, I don't think it is you. I don't understand. I thought you enjoyed coming out of your chrysalis and emerging into the light.'

Grey eyes the colour of a summer storm flashed at him. 'Don't presume to know me, Linton, because you don't have a clue who I really am.' She took a long slug of her coffee and then breathed in deeply, her breasts straining against her top.

His gaze immediately fell to her chest, seeking the image of creamy breasts from last night, which burned so brightly in his mind. Seeing an imagined image of her in a bikini top. Clearing his mind of everything except that. 'Come to Ledger's Gorge this afternoon and I can get to know you. We can swim up under the waterfall and—'

'No, thanks.' She pulled out the roster and slammed the filing-cabinet drawer closed.

The coolness of her voice whipped him. He shook his head, not quite believing he'd heard correctly. 'We don't have to swim. What about a walk?'

'No, thank you.'

Obviously he was missing something. Perhaps she wanted to have a say in the destination. 'What would you like to do?'

She tilted her pert chin upwards, as if slicing the air around it. 'Linton, I don't want to do anything with you except work.'

An alien emotion circled him. 'You're dumping me?'

Incredulity creased her brow. 'How can I be dumping you? We weren't even on a date. Besides, you're not known for a follow-up call and you're especially not known for a follow-up date, so you should be relieved.'

The barb hit him in a place usually so well protected that nothing penetrated. He ignored her comment, focusing on his need. He smiled a knowing smile. 'But you have to admit we had a great time together, especially on your veranda.' His voice deepened of its own accord. 'Don't you want to explore that further?'

Her eyes darkened to the colour of polished iron ore.

He knew that colour. A self-indulgent thought warmed him. Whatever was going on behind that blue hair, she couldn't deny the attraction that simmered between them.

Silver immediately glinted in the grey depths, flashing at him like the light from a welder's torch. The abrupt change, so unexpected, startled him.

She drew herself up onto the balls of her feet, her body almost vibrating. 'You've known me for a year, Linton. In all that time you've never seen me as anyone other than a reliable nurse who made your life easier. The *one* time I put on a slinky dress, you suddenly see me.'

Her voice trembled. 'Except that wasn't really me. I showed you what you wanted to see. You obviously prefer to see me that way but the problem is, I don't agree.' She hugged her arms around herself. 'I thought you understood me but I got that so wrong. Last night was all about *you* and nothing to do with me. You are so...so shallow. Everything I've every heard about you and wanted to ignore is true. You really are the playboy doctor. Well, sorry, I don't want to play.'

Her words cut and ripped, the truth stark and unrelenting. *I showed you what you wanted to see.* Anger surged in to soothe the pain. 'I have never pretended to be anything other than what I am. I have never made a promise I haven't kept.'

A flush of colour stained her cheeks. 'That doesn't make

you honourable.' She picked up the roster and, hugging it close to her chest, walked away from him.

His anger staggered under the weight of her accusation. He wanted to yell at her to come back, that she was wrong, that she knew nothing about him, but he kept hearing the same words over and over. *You are so shallow.*

He wasn't shallow. He was nothing like the man that had destroyed her confidence, telling her she was unattractive, telling her what to wear.

You told her what to wear.

No! His rage stampeded over the ugly thought. What he'd done had been totally different. It had been concern for her that had made him encourage her to come out from behind her baggy clothes and wear that dress. It had been the action of a friend.

But the memory of her taste, the touch of her lips against his, the feel of her head against his chest, the vision of her curvaceous body in that dress—all of it whipped him like a cat-o'-nine-tails.

Hell, a friend didn't kiss another friend to the point of exhaustion.

You've known me for a year, Linton.

What had he done? His head pounded and he rubbed his neck as he tried to make sense of it all.

The unpalatable truth trickled through him. Emily was right. He'd admired her as a nurse, he'd seen her as a mate and nothing more. Last night he'd let raging, unchecked hormones turn a friendship on its head. He'd let lust for her body ride roughshod over their camaraderie, totally ignoring the woman inside the gorgeous body. A woman who was still hurting and emotionally raw from the abuse she'd had levelled at her by her ex-boyfriend.

A sigh shuddered from his lungs. He'd been a total fool. Seducing a friend wasn't part of the friendship code.

With a startling clarity that made him sway, he realised he'd never had a female friend before.

Tamara?

No! Tamara hadn't been a friend. Tamara had been a self-serving schemer. He'd thought he'd married a partner for life but she hadn't actually wanted him. No, Tamara had never been a friend.

He thought of this morning, working with a cool and starchy Emily. A vision of that sort of relationship sent a shudder of loss through him. He missed her friendship already.

He jammed his hands in his coat pockets, his heart pounding hard. He'd messed this up because he had no idea how to be friends with a woman. He knew how to date, how to charm, how to get his own way, but he didn't have a clue about platonic friendship. That wasn't a lesson his father had taught him.

You are so shallow.

A metallic taste burned the back of his throat at her words, which had pierced with deadly accuracy.

He wanted Emily's friendship back. He wanted the companionship she'd offered, the teasing when he took himself too seriously, the shared laughs. He wanted all of it.

He'd just have to show her he was nothing like that man she'd left and he was a lot deeper than she thought he was.

CHAPTER EIGHT

THE pages in the book blurred and Emily's wrist ached from the copious notes she'd written. Five cold cups of tea cluttered the desk and she could see right through the clear bottom of the glass bowl holding bright-coloured chocolate lollies. She had to keep focused to have all the required course work for her Master's done by the time her residential week arrived. And it was scarily close.

'Em, it's five o'clock.' Jim banged on the Woollara Station's office door before opening it and poking his head around. 'I think you've done enough for the day. The sun's setting, it's officially Saturday night, the lamb's roasting in the oven and Hayden just rang. He, Nadine and the kids are coming over.'

'Thanks, Dad. I'll come and set the table for you.'

'I've done that. You can shell the peas and talk to me while I make the gravy.' He gave her a fatherly smile.

'Deal. I'll be there in five.' Emily closed her books. She'd been working all day on her Master's, retreating to the office for peace and quiet, but now she was ready to stop.

She hadn't seen her middle brother and his family for a few weeks and baby Alby would have changed so much.

Anticipating an enjoyable evening, she hummed to herself as she returned her father's desk to its usual neat state.

Family dinners were always fun. She and Mark were the only siblings still living at home. Stuart and Eric shared bachelor quarters down by the shearing shed and Hayden and Nadine's house was one hundred kilometres away on the northern boundary.

But when word got out that Jim was cooking a roast, it was amazing how many of her brothers appeared in the kitchen, and they usually brought a few mates with them. Still, it *was* Saturday night and Eric and Stuart had gone into Warragurra to the rugby match so she didn't expect them to be coming.

That meant more time with Hayden and Nadine and more cuddles with her nephews. After the week she'd had she could do with a bit of family time. It would be a lot less complicated than work. Last Sunday morning had changed everything between her and Linton. Actually, the ball had changed everything between her and Linton.

A sigh shuddered through her. She still hated that she'd let stars in her eyes dazzle and blind her, affecting her judgement. When she'd seen the way Linton had gazed at her on Sunday morning, as if he could see through her clothes, she had known that the decision she'd made in the early hours of that morning had been the right one.

A hard one, but the right one.

At the moment she didn't know which was worse—the blatant desire in Linton's eyes or memories of the bitter derision of Nathan's words. Both of them had wanted to mould her into something that wasn't her.

She acknowledged that in a way she'd let both men try and change her, but all of that was over now. She wasn't going to think about Linton any more, because when she did her heart pounded in anger and then beat quietly in sadness, leaving her totally confused.

She straightened her shoulders as she switched off the office light. She was older and wiser now. She and men didn't match. Right now she needed to focus on herself, work, her Master's and enjoy her extended family.

She made her way across the yard with a dog for company, and the low bellow of cattle competing with the raucous screech of the yellow-crested cockatoos nesting for the night. Two kangaroos bounded near the far fence, the fading light sending them to the shelter of the trees down by the river, the twinkling light of the evening star guiding their way.

As she drew level with the house, a four-wheel-drive pulled up, the tyres crunching on the gravel. A three-year-old boy tumbled out and raced toward her, his blond hair flying. 'Emily!'

'Tyler!' She swooped him up in her arms and spun him around.

Squeals of delight showered over her.

'Hey, sis, you're looking good.' Hayden gave her a kiss on the cheek and a questioning look. 'Been shopping?'

Experimenting with new clothes was part of working out her very own style, one she was choosing for herself. Not too revealing but not sacks either, she'd been enjoying the process.

She put a squirming Tyler down and watched him run toward the house, ignoring her brother's gaze. 'I might have.'

'About time.' Hayden spoke matter-of-factly. 'You should burn those horrible baggy shirts.'

'Shut up.' She playfully elbowed her brother in the ribs. Of all her brothers, Hayden knew her best.

Hayden caught her in a headlock.

'Play nice, you two.' Nadine's gentle voice interrupted their horseplay.

'Oh, can I cuddle Alby?' Emily put out her arms for the baby.

His mother smiled a tired smile. 'You can cuddle him for as long as you like.'

The bang of the wire door made them look up. Tyler stood on the back veranda with his hands on his hips, looking as self-important as a pre-schooler could look. 'Granddad says peas need shelling and I can help 'cos I'm a fwee-year-old.'

'That you are, mate.' Hayden bounded up the steps and raced him into the house.

The aroma of roasting lamb and garlic wafted over Emily as soon as she entered the kitchen. A big metal bowl sat in the middle of the table filled with pea pods, freshly picked from the home-paddock garden. Tyler climbed up onto a stool and Hayden sat next to him, demonstrating how to shell the peas.

'Hey, do you remember the time we ate so many peas while we were picking them that there were none for dinner?' Hayden grinned at Emily.

She laughed. 'Mum was furious because the circuit magistrate was coming to dinner that night and there were no green vegetables.'

Jim poured a generous slurp of red wine into the gravy, his deep, rumbling voice joining the laughter. 'Your mother was trying to outcook Mrs Sanderson, who'd fed him the night before. You two put her reputation as the district's best cook on the line.'

The laughter and warmth of the kitchen encircled them, relaxing Emily. She cuddled the baby, breathing in the sweet milky smell. A long-held dream of a baby of her own hovered briefly before she dismissed it as nonsense. She wanted a child but not without a husband. Right now the chances of that ever happening were zero to nothing. She really had to learn how to pick the right guy.

She glanced up and watched Nadine and Hayden teaching their son how to shell peas while Jim poured drinks and stirred the gravy. Everyone devoured the pre-dinner pesto dip and almost all of Tyler's chips, much to his chagrin.

'Granddad said they were for me.' He mutinously moved the bowl to the side.

His father moved it back. 'Sharing the chips is the right thing to do, mate.'

Tyler's bottom lip wobbled.

'Right, then. I'm almost ready to carve and dish up.' Jim clapped his hands.

The wire door banged. 'That's perfect timing, Dad. Hope you've cooked the usual big one.' Stuart strode into the kitchen, his cheeks ruddy from the evening chill.

'What happened to the post-match celebrations?' Emily raised her head from admiring the perfect shape of Alby's tiny ears.

Stuart grinned. 'Dad's cooking a lamb roast, sis. I never miss that.'

'How much did Warragurra lose by?' Jim clapped his hand on his youngest son's shoulder.

A sheepish expression crossed Stuart's face. 'We're missing Ben McCreedy. We came in for a drubbing, fifty-seven ten. Combine that woeful score with the rain and the crush at the Royal, and Eric and I thought we'd come home for some family fun.'

'Hey, Dad.' Eric's stocky bulk crossed the threshold and he immediately moved away from the door. A tall man stood in the shadow of the dark veranda. 'You remember Linton. We thought he looked like he could do with a feed.'

Emily's knees buckled as she clutched Alby tightly against her. Linton stood tall and solid, filling the doorway, a smile on his handsome face, a Warragurra Roosters' scarf around his neck, his brown hair ruffled by the wind and his long legs clad in tight blue denim.

Casual, gorgeous and all male.

She swallowed a groan as a traitorous swirl of heat wound through her. Of all the men her brothers could have run into at the match and invited home, why did it have to be Linton?

Her vision of a relaxed family evening vaporised before her eyes.

'Come in, Linton.' Jim's voice boomed. 'Dinner's almost on the table. Choose yourself a seat.'

Linton shook Emily's father's hand. 'Are you sure?'

'Absolutely. The boys are always bringing home extras and there's plenty.' He plunged a carving fork into the leg of lamb. 'Emily, Linton hasn't met Hayden and Nadine.'

Linton caught the ripple of tension across her shoulders. He'd spied Emily the moment Eric had moved away from the door. If the truth be told, he'd been searching for her the moment he'd looked into the room. His blood warmed at the sight of her, even though once again he hardly recognised her.

Her hair was no longer blue but a warm honey blonde. The soft curls brushed her shoulders, tickling the fine wool of her chocolate-brown V-necked sweater, which contrasted with a finely striped shirt with white collar and cuffs. Low-rise cords, the grey-brown colour of the bush wallaby, hugged her hips.

Country chic.

Totally gorgeous. His gut kicked as desire rolled it over. He immediately stomped on it. *Think friend.* Emily was his colleague and hopefully soon-to-be-again friend. He'd only accepted Eric's invitation to dinner because he'd thought it would be an opportunity to show Emily a completely different side of him.

A and E had been frantic lately and there hadn't been any time to talk to her about anything other than patients. He doubted she would have accepted an invitation for coffee, lunch or dinner, even if he had offered.

All week at work she'd had bright blue hair and a pale face. She'd been steely professional, only seeking him out about work-related issues. Yet now, surrounded by her family, the prickly woman was gone and she glowed in the warm earthy colours that suited her so well. He hardly recognised her but it wasn't just the clothes or the hair. Something about her was different, he just couldn't quite pin down what.

She held his gaze for an infinitesimal moment, her expression questioning, before she laid the baby in the pram. Straightening up, she spoke briskly, as if she was at work. 'Linton, I'd like you to meet my middle brother, Hayden, his wife Nadine—'

'And me!' A little boy tugged at her sweater.

The starchy Emily evaporated, her face creasing in laughter lines as she bobbed down and picked up the child. 'And Tyler.'

Tyler leaned out of her arms toward the pram. 'And that's my baby brother.' The pride in his voice was unmistakable.

A strange sensation washed over Linton. He didn't want to call it loneliness. He moved forward, his arm extended as Hayden rose to his feet. 'Great to meet you. Emily didn't mention she was an auntie.'

'She's probably too busy bossing you around at work.' Hayden grinned as he shook Linton's hand.

The welcome in Hayden's grip relaxed him. 'She's been known to have an organising moment or two.'

'I do *not* boss.' Emily sat Tyler on his chair.

Her brother gave a snort and turned toward his sister. 'Yeah, right, and pigs might fly. You've been bossy since the moment you were born.' He turned back to Linton, rolling his eyes. 'When she gets a bee in her bonnet, she's legendary. Once she turned this kitchen into a production line. She had all of us boys preserving fruit and baking cakes to enter in the Warragurra Show. Eric in an apron was a sight to behold.'

'I publicly thanked you for your contribution when I won first prize.' Emily slid onto her chair.

'And I'm still wearing *that* down at the clubrooms.' Hayden tied a bib around Tyler's neck.

'I was just helping you get in touch with your feminine side, so you should be thanking me because, if I remember, it was after that show that Nadine noticed you.' Emily shot Hayden a triumphant look, her chin tilted skyward.

'Nadine noticed me because of my spectacular riding skills at the rodeo.'

'The time the bull bucked you and you went to hospital?'

Nadine patted a chair with her hand. 'Sit down, Linton, and just ignore them. This is what they do.'

Linton sat down and put his serviette on his knee. 'So was it the cooking or the riding of the bull that made you notice Hayden?'

The young wife smiled a knowing smile. 'Actually, it was his enthusiasm and total commitment to whatever he takes on. This family has that in spades.'

Linton surreptitiously glanced at Emily, immediately recognising what Nadine meant.

Eric and Stuart joined them, adding their stories about

Emily bossing them around, the loving banter obvious in their voices.

Jim carved the meat and plates were passed down the long table. Outstretched arms reached and received the dishes of roast vegetables and peas, and mint jelly was generously dobbed on top of the thick gravy. Glasses clinked, cutlery scraped against the blue and white china, and the satisfied sounds of a group of people eating good food echoed around the kitchen.

'I think we should send a hundred head of cattle down to the sale yards next week.' Hayden reached for the salt.

'Mark, have you met the new kindergarten teacher?' Nadine casually picked up the pepper grinder.

The bachelor shifted uncomfortably in his seat and looked at Hayden. 'So are you going to muster on Tuesday?'

Eric waved his fork. 'You should ask her out, bro.'

'Linton, I was reading in the *New Scientist* about surgeons using scorpion toxin to highlight malignant cells.' Jim's blue eyes burned with intelligence and hospitality.

Linton opened his mouth to reply.

'I made these peas, Granddad.'

'And you did a great job, buddy.' Jim handed the pre-schooler a spoon. 'But how about using this, rather than your fingers?'

'Did anyone read about the latest report on salinity?' Emily voiced the question into the congested air.

Mark attempted to stick to one topic. 'Dad, will you be mustering with us on Tuesday?'

'Mark can you fix the pump on the boundary dam sooner rather than later?' Stuart scooped more potatoes onto his plate.

'And when you've done that, you can call into the kinder

and fix the pump on the rainwater tank. I tried but you're better at that sort of thing.' Hayden shot his brother a wicked grin. 'Hey, Tyler, you'd like Uncle Mark to come and visit you at kinder, wouldn't you?'

The little boy's blue eyes widened in delight. 'I can show him the walking fish.'

Linton's brain whirled as he tried to grab onto a conversation but found it had immediately morphed into something different. He caught Emily's twinkling gaze, her eyes dancing with laughter at what he knew must be a completely bewildered expression on his face.

He mouthed, 'Is it always like this?'

She nodded and asked her question about the salinity report again.

This time Jim replied, and Linton realised that in conversations at this table it was survival of the fittest. Whoever talked loudest and more often got heard. The memory of dinners past in his childhood homes floated through his mind.

The quiet meals with his mother and Cliff, often focused on earnest political discussions, which had contrasted dramatically with meals at his father's house. The large modern glass and granite table had often been filled with strangers— women who had been trying to impress his father by mothering Linton. Women his father had had no plan on seeing a second or third time.

Once he'd left home, many meals had been spent at the hospital talking shop, or cooking for one at his own place, and more recently out at restaurants on dates, having the usual 'getting to know you' conversations.

All of those meals had lacked the warmth, vitality, competitiveness and camaraderie of this table. He had a sense of having missed out on something special in his family homes. His bewilderment suddenly vanished and everything became clear. He wanted to be part of it, he wanted to be in on this chaotic conversation, and at the same time he could show Emily that he wasn't the shallow womaniser she'd tagged him as.

He projected his voice into the melee. 'Scorpion toxin is fluorescent so it outlines the boundary of the malignant tumour.'

Jim nodded. 'Nature's amazing, isn't it?'

Eric spluttered. 'Amazing? It's a right pain. Those kangaroos knocked over the river paddock fence *again*.'

Emily squirted green liquid detergent into the sink and started to attack the large pile of dishes now that everyone had consumed more sticky toffee pudding than was probably good for them. It felt good to be doing *something*, rather than just sitting and wondering why Linton was here. Why was he casually leaning back in a chair at her father's table, looking for the entire world like he belonged there?

He even sounded liked he belonged. He'd matched her brothers in their verbal sparring debates that were synonymous with family meals, as well as taking a genuine interest in everyone, actively drawing them out, seeking their opinions.

And he did it with such casual ease, looking completely and utterly, devastatingly gorgeous. The "shallow man" accusation she'd hurled at him almost a week ago seemed grossly unfair today.

She silently screamed as confusion encircled her. She wanted to run to the woolshed, just like when she'd been a little girl. Home was supposed to be a sanctuary from the world—a Linton-free zone.

Instead, her heart had been skipping beats all night, making her feel giddy. It had completely ignored every reasonable request she'd made of it to beat normally and treat Linton like any other guest. Every nerve pulled taut, ready to snap, and she just wished Linton would go home so she could find her equilibrium again.

Not that he'd really talked to her. He'd been busy chatting with everyone else. He'd even made an effort with Tyler. It rankled that she felt ignored. She shouldn't care.

Voices from the table drifted over to her and she heard snatches of conversation and her father discussing the Warragurra Rodeo, which was going to be held the following weekend.

'Where are the teatowels kept?' Linton's deep voice unexpectedly rumbled behind her.

A strong tingling wave washed through her. Angry with herself, she snapped, asking the question that had bugged her all night. 'Why are you here?'

His green eyes flickered with darker shards of green, giving her a look that made her feel small and mean. 'Your brothers invited me.'

He reached around her and grabbed a teatowel, his heat slamming into her. He dropped his voice so only she could hear. 'You look great, by the way.'

She plunged a bowl under the white suds and vigorously scrubbed it with the brush, trying to stop the sensation of lightness sweeping through her. She didn't want to enjoy the compliment. She was furious with him. She breathed out a strained but polite 'Thanks'.

'Your dad reads pretty widely.' His strong, tanned hands dextrously wiped a plate dry.

'What, for a farmer?' Suds sprayed her in disapproval.

He raised his brows in question. 'Emily, do you have a problem with me being here?'

Yes! Yes, I do. But she couldn't say that. He was the guest of her brothers, although why he'd want to be here after she'd called him shallow she had no idea.

Anger meshed with longing, need duelled with frustration. He had no right to look so at home in her family kitchen! Not when he'd hurt her so much. She paused, her gloved hands resting on the sink, and pulled in a deep breath. 'I'm sorry, that was rude. I've been studying all day and I'm tired and scratchy.'

'Study does that.' He gave a nod of understanding. 'I've been thinking about what you said the other day.' He pushed the teatowel deep into the glass and looked thoughtful. 'You were right. I was pretty shallow and I hurt your feelings and abused your friendship. Our friendship.' He caught her gaze, his eyes serious. 'Sorry.'

Had she been holding a plate, it would have slipped from her fingers. She gripped the edge of the sink for support as her knees sagged. So that was why he was here—he'd come to apologise. She hadn't expected that at all. Nathan had *never* apologised, he'd only blamed.

'You want to be friends?' She couldn't hide the disbelief in her voice.

Contrition interplayed with hesitancy. 'I do. I think we can do that, don't you?'

'Colleagues and friends?' She must sound completely vacant, repeating everything he'd said, but her mind continued to be blank, unable to absorb this astonishing turnaround.

He nodded. 'Friends and colleagues.'

She rolled the idea around in her head. This meant they could start afresh with no confusion. The crazy desire that had simmered between them would disappear now they had ground rules. They were workmates and friends, pure and simple. They'd never socialised together before the ball so there was no reason to expect that to change.

Everything was moving forward to a new and improved working relationship. She couldn't stop herself from smiling broadly. 'Apology accepted. Here's to the new order.' And she handed him a dripping pile of cutlery.

'Hey, Linton.' Stuart and Mark pushed their chairs back from the table. 'You ever been to a rodeo?'

Linton opened the drawer and dropped the cutlery into the slots as he dried each item. 'No, no yet.'

'Mate, you can't go back to Sydney before you've experienced a rodeo.' Eric appealed to Emily. 'Can he, sis?'

Three sets of eyes stared at her as her heart leapt into her mouth. What Eric was really saying was that the Tippett family would take Linton as their guest. And as all her brothers and her father would be involved in riding horses and roping bulls, that meant she would be the host. She would be the one spending all of Saturday with Linton.

Linton away from work was a totally different proposition. Dread danced with a sensation she refused to name.

She stared back at her brothers' questioning eyes. They had her on toast.

She gulped in a breath, playing the only card she had. 'Linton's pretty busy. I doubt he'd want to spend a day in the dust, watching you guys play around trying to prove you're men.' She turned back to the sink.

Linton flicked his teatowel like a whip. 'I'd love to go.'

Four small words sealed her fate.

CHAPTER NINE

EMILY checked the message on her phone for the third time. *Meet you by the stables. Linton.* But she couldn't see him anywhere.

She scanned the crowd again. Cowboys and cowgirls promenaded in their best jeans. Fitted button-down shirts in every colour of the rainbow were tucked neatly behind ornate belt buckles, which sparkled in the sunshine, and showed off a wide variety of waistlines. A hat graced every head, some tipped forward, some tipped back and some hung against their owners' backs, flicked off by the occasional gust of wind that sent dust and leaves swirling into the air.

Linton should have stood out in the crowd because he didn't own any western gear. He was a city boy through and through. A city boy with a penchant for all things Italian.

'There you are. I thought I must have missed you.' Linton's hand caught her arm.

She spun around, his touch making her dizzy, the rich timbre of his voice making her heart skip. She gazed up at him, blinking rapidly. 'Linton?'

He flicked his thumbs into the belt hooks of his moleskins and threw his shoulders back, standing tall, his chest straining the fabric of his jade-coloured shirt.

She forgot to breathe.

Then he grinned, his eyes flashing, and he tipped his hat. 'Ma'am.'

A giggle bubbled up, escaping through her lips.

'Hey, the salesman at Country Outfitters said this was the gear I needed.' Indignation clung to his words. 'I thought I looked like a pretty good cowboy.'

You look sensational. Good enough to eat. 'You look like a stockman.'

'Why not a cowboy?' He sounded like a little boy who had lost the costume competition.

'Denim is the cowboy code and you're in moleskins, which is the fabric of choice for drovers, stockmen, graziers and shearers. You'd better watch out—Dad might offer you a job. How are your roping skills?'

'I lassoed a pretty good nurse for the afternoon.' He slipped his hand against hers, his lean fingers closing around her finer ones. 'So, this is a rodeo. Busy, isn't it? Your brothers told me all about the camp drafting, which is on at four, so can you take me there?'

His wide palm engulfed her small hand, stealing all coherent thought. She stole a glance at him but his expression gave nothing much away. Smile lines creased the edges of his eyes and he looked happy, interested and laid-back.

All week at work he'd been affable and relaxed. She'd noticed little things like how he'd brought her a drink when he'd made one, how he'd asked if Mark had gone to kinder to see Tyler's Mexican walking fish and if she'd finished her first assignment for uni.

And, unlike with Nathan, none of it had come with a condition.

Instead, all of it had been the action of a friend doing the sorts of things that friends did for each other. And they'd talked about all sorts of things and laughed about nonsense. They'd become friends. Good friends. She believed he really did enjoy her company—in fact, at times he sought her out just to talk. Their friendship seemed to be working well for both of them.

It's harder than you thought.

She ignored the voice. Friendship was what they both wanted and it would be perfect if she could only ditch these irrational shimmers of sensation whenever he came near. They were supposed to have gone, banished by their friendship pact.

But they kept popping up to haunt her, like right now. She hauled in a deep breath, trying to settle her somersaulting stomach. The only reason he was holding her hand was so he didn't lose her in the crowd. She took a step and tugged his hand. 'If we go to the arena now, you can see some bull riding.'

Linton stood still, frowning. 'Please, tell me none of your brothers do that.'

'They all tried it once, Hayden even twice, but fortunately their skills lie on the back of a horse and camp drafting is a lot safer.' She tugged on his hand again. 'Come on, you need to get some red dust on those boots of yours so you don't look like such a city slicker.'

He counter-tugged, managing to move her slightly behind him as he strode off, his long legs quickly eating up the distance. 'I've been here for over a year, you know.'

She jogged to keep up. 'Mate, even if you married a local girl, settled down and had children and grandchildren...'

A horrified look streaked across his face at her words.

Half of her wanted to laugh and half of her wanted to cry. She forced herself to continue, 'You'd still be a city bloke, but your great-grandchildren would be locals.'

'That's never going to happen.'

His emphatic words pierced her like tiny arrows. 'What? Having grandchildren or marrying a local girl?' She worked hard to keep her tone light.

'Neither.' He took a sharp left, following the sign to the arena.

She stopped walking, dismay for him thundering through her. Even though she knew that they would never work as a couple, she'd assumed that at some point in the future he would marry. 'So even when you're back in Sydney, on track with your career plan of being in charge of a city hospital A and E, you still have no plans to marry?'

'No.' Determined, clear green eyes stared down at her. 'I tried it once.'

She stared at him, speechless, her brain refusing to work. 'You...you've been married?' She couldn't hide the shock in her voice.

He shrugged. 'We all make mistakes.'

She tugged him over to one side, out of the main thorough-fare. 'You've never said anything about being married.' She blurted out the words, stunned at his casual mention of such a big issue. Didn't friends tell each other things like that?

Tension radiated along his jaw. 'I was young and stupid. I'm divorced now.' The words rushed out stilted and defiant.

She stared at him, seeing a steely resentment she'd never really glimpsed before. Was this tied up with the playboy doctor? The need to know burned inside her but she wasn't certain he'd tell her. She gave it a shot. 'With my disastrous attempt at an adult relationship, I'm hardly in a position to judge you.'

His gaze wavered for a moment and then he spoke, his voice flat and devoid of emotion, as if he was telling a tale he'd told too many times before. 'From the age of twelve my father told me how much his life had improved once he'd divorced my mother. I hated hearing that and I used to daydream about happy families, and how I would fall in love and get married one day and *stay* married.'

'That sounds pretty normal.' She'd daydreamed the same sort of thing. In weaker moments she still did.

He snorted. 'Yeah, well, it's not normal for the Gregory men.' He ran his hand across the back of his neck. 'I met Tamara at a party when I was a fifth-year med student. She was majoring in literature and her student life was very different from mine. She went to plays, parties and poetry readings, and enjoyed campus life, while I was strapped to a horrendous study load. She'd call by the residence and drag me out and for the first time in a long time I had fun.' A grimace crossed his face. 'I completely missed that she had an agenda.'

She nodded her understanding, thinking of Nathan. 'Looks like we share that in common.'

His mouth twitched into a half-smile. 'I guess so. Anyway, my father wasn't happy about the amount of time I was spending with Tamara and he had her sussed much better than I did. But I was twenty-three, not a kid, and the more he pushed for us to break up, the more I pulled the other way. Tamara was keen to get married and I was determined to show Dad he was completely wrong about marriage.'

She thought of her parents, and of Nadine and Hayden. 'There's every chance he's wrong.'

Contempt instantly filled his face. 'No, Dad was spot on. Tamara and I lasted less than six months. Turns out she desperately wanted to be married to a doctor, only she'd picked the wrong one to suit her purposes. She didn't want the lifestyle that goes with an intern working sixty-plus hours a week, so she conveniently found herself another doctor—older, richer and further up the career ladder.'

The hurt in his voice was like a knife in her chest and her hand briefly stroked his arm, wanting to lessen his pain. 'She walked away from a good man.'

He shrugged off her words. 'It taught me a valuable lesson and now I listen to my father. I don't do long-term relationships and I won't ever let another woman put me in that position. I will never get married again.'

His matter-of-fact tone tinged with bitterness crashed down on her like a lead weight. *I will never get married again.* His words bellowed in her head and crazily part of her heart ripped slightly as her stomach unexpectedly tipped upside down.

Nausea rose upwards, almost making her gag.

His hand touched her arm. 'Are you OK? You look a bit white.'

She stepped back slightly, breaking the contact. 'I don't think I should have had that fried chicken from the snack bar.'

Instantly concern etched his face. 'Are you up to this rodeo?'

She gave herself a shake and plastered a smile on her lips. 'Absolutely. We can't have you going back to Sydney next year without experiencing the quintessential outback event.'

She marched toward the arena, wishing she could ride on a bucking bull. It would be a hell of a lot safer than dealing with Linton's personal bombshells.

Linton flinched every time a cowboy hit the dirt, bucked off a raging bull within seconds of being released from the pen. Emily had doggedly pushed through the crowd and she stood on the third rung of the blue temporary railing, while he stood slightly below her, his feet firmly on the ground. They were so close to the action that dust clogged his nostrils.

She called down to him. 'The cowboy needs to sit over his hand. If he leans back he can be whipped forward as the bull bucks. He doesn't want to do that because he can collide with the horns.' Emily pointed to the current rider who stayed seated using his posture and the power of his thighs to grip the beast.

Even through the dust and the aroma of the animals, her perfume taunted him. He should be transfixed by the skill of the cowboys on the bulls, but he kept sneaking peeks at her. He hadn't expected her to be wearing a skirt today but the layered denim flared out around her knees every time she moved, flashing a hint of skin—the only bit of her skin visible before the rest of her shapely legs disappeared under the decorative leather of her knee-high boots. The floral motif in cream, pink and green hugged her calves before merging into stitched pink leather.

He'd never seen pink cowgirl boots before—they were distinctively Emily. She could wear the most unusual things with flair.

He flexed his fingers against the urge to rest his palm against the area of soft skin behind her knee. He closed his eyes against the image of creamy thighs.

Being friends with Emily was supposed to have flattened out his response to her. Lusting after friends wasn't acceptable and yet every time he slotted her into a safe hole, every time he pegged her down, she surprised him. She had more facets than crystal and every one of them intrigued him.

Bright, intelligent, funny and prosaic, he enjoyed every moment he spent with her. Since he'd apologised she'd seemed more relaxed around him and the last seven days had been one of the best weeks he'd spent in Warragurra.

One of the best weeks you've had anywhere.

He refused to acknowledge the thought. *She's just a friend.*

'No!' Emily's voice speared through him.

Surely he hadn't spoken his thoughts out loud?

A flash of blue and large expanse of pink suddenly pushed past him as Emily flung her leg over the railing.

He grabbed her, stalling her flight. 'What are you doing?' Irrational fear for her gripped his chest.

Her look of incredulity threw him and he quickly scanned the arena. A cowboy lay eerily still in the red dirt as the bull charged frantically round the ring.

He'd been so busy gazing at Emily he'd missed the moment the cowboy had been thrown.

His grip tightened around her thigh. 'You're not going in there until the bull has been penned, and then I'm coming with you.'

Her mouth flattened into a mulish line but she stayed still. 'The moment the first-aiders arrive we can go in.'

Seconds ticked by, lengthened by the impotence of not being able to act until the scene was safe and secured. Finally, the bull disappeared into the pen, the gate closing firmly behind it.

'Now.' Emily shook off Linton's hand and jumped down, a plume of red dust rising behind her.

He hurdled the railing and quickly followed.

They crossed the wide arena, arriving at the cowboy just as the first-aid workers arrived.

'Good to see you, Doc.' Ash, one of the first-aiders, immediately handed over his kit, relief clear on his face.

'Troy, where does it hurt?' Emily's hands started to open the cowboy's shirt, looking for injury.

'I thought I was free, I thought I was clear, but then he

tossed me and caught me on the leg.' Troy struggled, trying
to sit up, but fell back in pain.

'I need the scissors.'

Ash handed her a pair of shears and with precision born
of experience she quickly cut the cowboy's jeans straight
up the front.

Linton's gut heaved as he registered the extent of the injury
on Troy's leg. The bull's horn had entered his leg, piercing the
skin, with an entry and an exit wound. The leg lay at a strange
angle to its partner, a sure sign of a fracture. 'Did it trample
you?'

'Nah, I managed to roll away.'

'You're damn lucky.'

He caught Emily's relieved expression and nodded. If the
hoof or horn of a five-hundred-kilogram bull had connected
with Troy's chest or abdomen, there was every chance the
cowboy would now be dead.

He turned his attention back to the leg while Emily
wrapped a tourniquet around Troy's arm. 'The anterior tibia
artery and the peroneal artery run pretty close to this puncture
wound. What's his BP like?'

'One hundred on sixty.' Emily chewed her bottom lip. 'Is
he bleeding into his leg?'

Linton pressed his fingers on the top of Troy's foot, feeling
for the pedal pulse, which was weak and thready. 'He's lucky
Warragurra Base is only a ten-minute ambulance ride away
or I would have to make a fasciotomy incision to release the
trapped blood and relieve the pressure.'

'Will my leg be OK?' Troy's voice wobbled.

Linton sighed. 'I'm pretty certain you've fractured your
fibula, one of the bones in your lower leg. I'm worried about
nerve damage and infection so the sooner we get you to

Warragurra Base and under the care of Jeremy Fallon, the better.'

'Em, I'm really thirsty.' The young man's face was covered in dirt.

Emily swiftly inserted the IV. 'Troy, you'll be going to the operating theatre so I can't give you anything to drink, but you can rinse your mouth.'

Ash handed her a water bottle and together they helped Troy rinse and spit.

Using sterile gauze and saline, Linton cleaned and covered the puncture wounds before sliding an inflatable splint onto Troy's lower leg. 'As soon as you're at the hospital we'll give you a tetanus shot and a huge amount of antibiotics.'

The dazed cowboy nodded vaguely, shock starting to catch up with him.

The piercing siren of the ambulance heralded its arrival. Andrew and fellow paramedic Pete jumped out and opened the back door.

Emily jogged over to assist.

Linton looked up just as Andrew's arm slid around her waist for an instant as he leaned in to greet her.

Green rage stabbed him in the chest so hard he gasped. His legs tensed as if to propel him up from his squatting position like a runner in the blocks, to project him over to place himself firmly between Andrew and Emily.

His hands shook on the splint. He breathed deeply, focusing on the job like it was a lifeline. None of this made any sense. If he'd learned one thing in the last two weeks it was that he wouldn't let anything compromise his friendship with Emily.

Especially lust. He'd almost messed things up once and he wouldn't risk that happening again. Emily was his nurse, his friend and his good mate.

Besides, Emily was a country girl who deserved to marry a guy who wanted a rural life and a tribe of kids. He didn't want any of that.

Friendship was what they both wanted, what they had agreed on.

She called his name and he looked up into silver-grey eyes full of concern for their patient but backlit with a simmering heat. A heat he instantly recognised. A heat he knew he matched.

A fireball of lust exploded in his chest, matching the heat of desire and naked need in her eyes.

A need they had for each other. A need their friendship hadn't diminished one tiny bit. If anything, it had increased it, ramping it up to a raging inferno.

Emily cleared her throat and tossed her head, forcing down the thunderous wave of molten craving for Linton that had suddenly exploded inside her when he'd caught her gaze. He'd stared so deeply into her eyes she could have sworn he'd seen her soul. 'Um, Andrew and Pete want to know if you're riding back to the hospital with Troy?'

Linton stood up. 'If Jeremy can meet the ambulance at the hospital, I won't have to go back. Troy's vital signs are stable for travel, Pete and Andrew are the most experienced paramedics and Daniel is more than capable of doing the pre-op stuff. I'll talk to Jeremy now.' He punched a number into his phone and then hailed Andrew to bring the stretcher.

Andrew dropped down next to their patient. 'Right, Troy, we're going to transfer you now. Can you lift yourself up on your arms? Pete and I will help you.' He put his arms under Troy's.

Emily controlled Troy's legs.

'On my count. One, two, three…' Andrew grunted.

A moment later Troy was lying on the stretcher, his face pale and sweaty. 'I'd rather be riding the bull.'

'You'll be feeling a lot better in a few hours.' Emily patted his arm.

Troy grabbed her hand. 'Eric's kept pretty quiet about his stunning sister. How about a date?'

'Get in line,' Andrew quipped, but his expression stayed serious.

Emily laughed and extricated her hand from Troy's. 'Ask me when you can dance on both legs, cowboy.' She waved, floating on the compliments as Andrew and Pete started to push the stretcher toward the rig.

'Ask you what?' Linton's breath caressed her ear, his brown hair brushing hers as he leaned in close.

She gave a self-conscious laugh to cover her hammering heart. 'Troy's high on painkillers and wants to ask me out on a date.'

Linton grunted as his arm snaked around her waist. 'Come on, we have to get out of the arena.' He ushered her across to the nearest gate.

She fully expected his arm to drop away the moment they were on the spectators' side of the gate but he left it there, the touch casually light but, oh, so wonderful. 'I gather Jeremy is at the hospital.'

'Yep, which means you can continue with showing me the rodeo.'

A crazy feeling of relief ricocheted through her. She shouldn't care so much that he was staying, but she did.

'Emmie! Emmie!'

Emily looked around but couldn't see who was calling her name. Suddenly, a pair of arms wrapped themselves around her knees. 'Tyler.' She tousled his hair. 'Where's Mummy?'

Linton moved away and Emily saw him relieve Nadine of the pram.

Her sister-in-law gave a weary smile. 'I hear you've both had a bit of excitement.'

'I saw the ambulance's red flashing lights,' Tyler announced proudly. 'Now I'm going to watch Daddy get the heifer to run around like the number eight.'

'If we can ever get close enough.' Nadine sighed as the crowd surged around them.

'I think I can help with that.' Linton bent down to Tyler's height. 'Would you like a ride on my shoulders so you can see?'

Tyler glanced at Nadine, who nodded.

'Yes, please!'

Linton hoisted the almost four-year-old up onto his shoulders.

Tyler yelled out, 'Yee-hah' and pretended to crack a whip.

Linton attempted to whinny.

Emily bit her lip as she caught the enthusiastic grins on both the big boy's and the little boy's faces. Yet this was the man who didn't want to marry and have children. Did he have any clue what he was going to miss out on by not being a father?

'Having fun?' Nadine asked softly, her brown eyes seeing far too much.

'More fun than Troy.' She quickly followed Linton, making way for the pram and avoiding a conversation she didn't want to have with her sister-in-law.

Nadine found a place to sit so she could feed Alby, and Emily and Linton safely flanked the enthusiastic Tyler on the rails. Cheering, they watched closely as all the Tippett men manoeuvred their horses through their paces.

'They're so fast.' Admiration vibrated through Linton's voice.

She smiled at his interest. 'They need to be. I know a lot of mustering gets done by helicopter these days but a good stockman and his horse are invaluable. There are plenty of times when you have to cut a beast out from the mob and send it into the stockyard.'

'They don't seem to like being separated.' Linton pointed to Hayden as he wielded his horse around to drive the heifer away from the mob.

'It's a natural instinct to return to the safety of the mob. Bit like humans really. What you know seems safest, but it's not what is necessarily best for you.'

He tilted his head and studied her for a moment. 'Like how for the last few years you've been trying to be the person you think people want you to be rather than being true to yourself?' His gaze shot precise darts. 'Like dyeing your hair when everything gets too much for you?'

Air whooshed out of her lungs as if they'd been punctured. She gripped the railing, her head spinning. He'd worked it out—the connection between how she was feeling and her hair. His intuition scared her. It was like being stripped naked in front of him and being completely on show.

She defiantly lifted her chin, grappling to regain her composure. 'Actually, I was thinking more of you. How you're scared of letting yourself get close to anyone again so you date and move on. It sounds lonely to me, and doesn't it get tiring?'

'I'm close to plenty of people.' Emerald eyes flashed angrily and deep furrows creased his brow. 'I know what works for me and relationships don't. I have the right to make that choice.'

'Look!' Tyler pulled on Linton's sleeve, breaking the moment as Eric rode in on his new horse, rider and beast moving almost in unison. He jumped on the rails in excitement. 'Uncle Eric said he's going to win.'

Emily studied the horse's reactions to her brother's touch, part of her thankful, part of her frustrated, that the difficult conversation had just been cut short. 'I think he needs a bit more time to get to know his horse and then he could be unbeatable.'

Linton slid his hand on the little boy's back, pushing him gently against the rails to keep him safe. 'I think it would be great if a Tippett won. Maybe one day you'll be out there.'

'Of course I will be.'

Linton grinned. 'Good to see a man who knows his mind.'

They watched the rest of the competition and then all the Tippett men joined them, Hayden victorious with the winner's cup and Eric agreeably accepting second place.

'But watch your back, bro. Next year that cup is mine.'

Laughter and banter carried in the air as dusk fell quickly. The stars rose and twinkled in the night sky and the carnival part of the rodeo kicked off. Country and western music floated across the showgrounds; squeals and screams rent the air as heart-stopping, body-jolting, adrenaline-rushing rides spun and twirled, their lights merging into bright lines of red, green and blue.

The sideshow alley quickly filled with strolling couples and excited children. Cowboys showed off their skill with popguns, mowing down the moving metal ducks and claiming prizes for their girls. Children, sticky with fairy floss, fell asleep on their fathers' shoulders, the wonder of the day catching up with them. Nadine and Hayden gathered their children and headed off to the babysitter's, planning to return and enjoy an evening of grown-up fun, while the other Tippett men drifted off to the band tent.

Suddenly Linton's hand caught Emily's. 'Come on. Stuart tells me that if I want to be a cowboy, apart from being able to rope and tie, sit on a horse for twelve hours a day and wrestle a steer, I need to take a girl line-dancing.' He winked at her. 'And those pink boots of yours look like they can teach my boring brown ones to dance.'

Laughter threatened to tumble from her lips. Urbane Linton line-dancing was an impossible image. But she glimpsed the same sense of purpose in his eyes that he always wore at work, whether it was in the middle of an emergency or teaching the medical students.

Luxurious warmth flooded her. He was offering to go line-dancing because he thought it was what she wanted to do. He was a sincere, caring man, the polar opposite of Nathan. She didn't even want to compare the two of them because it was no contest at all.

When she'd lashed out at him after the ball it had been because she'd wanted him to see her for who she truly was, and today on the railings he'd told her with pinpoint accuracy that had seen and knew the real Emily. He was a great friend.

Sure, but he still wants you.

The heat and lust that had passed between them in the arena had left her in no doubt that he still desired her. Only this time it was different. This time she knew she meant more to him than just a curvaceous body.

And you want him.

She accepted the words without argument. Her defences against the overwhelming attraction she had for him had now crumbled to dust. Every time he stood near her she quivered with need. She wanted to be in his arms, she wanted his touch on every part of her body, she wanted…him. All of him.

And for the first time in her life she really knew what she wanted. She wanted what he was prepared to give—one night.

The acknowledgement of that truth sent a glorious sense of freedom through her. She was finally being true to herself. She didn't care what people would think, she didn't have to hide behind clothes or other people's opinions. She was no longer scared of disappointing someone, and if she did, well, it didn't matter.

Linton had looked at her today like no man had ever looked at her—with naked and consuming need.

And she wanted him with every part of herself.

He doesn't want a wife or family. You can't have sex and still be friends. The rational thoughts tried valiantly to implant themselves into her euphoria.

But she closed her mind to them. She was done with being sensible and cautious. She'd worry about all of that tomorrow. Right now she wanted to see that look in his eyes again. The look that said, 'I want you now.'

But she knew he wouldn't act on it because of the way she'd rejected his last attempt at seduction.

No, this time she would have to be the one to ask.

The idea thrilled and terrified her all at the same time.

CHAPTER TEN

'Um, isn't the line-dancing tent in the opposite direction?' Linton glanced around as Emily firmly dragged him away from sideshow alley, the sounds of the night receding into the distance.

Her left hand rested on her hip, her expression cheeky. 'No self-respecting cowboy learns to dance in public.' She turned toward the stables. 'I'll run you through the basic steps first, before unleashing you on an unsuspecting crowd.'

'Hey, I'm not that uncoordinated.' But his comment was lost in the noise of the old wooden door sliding open.

The sweet smell of hay wafted out to meet them, the aroma released by cool air meeting warm. Emily flicked on a light. The naked bulb struggled to emit a weak yellow glow. A horse neighed.

'Hey, Blossom, it's just me.'

She moved inside and stroked the horse's head as three other familiar-looking horses stirred from their rest, inquisitively looking to see who had entered their domain.

Linton followed, his eyes quickly adjusting to the gloom. 'Isn't that Eric's horse?' He recognised the distinctive patterned coat.

Emily smiled. 'Well spotted, Doctor. We might just make

a cowboy out of you yet. Welcome to the Tippett barn. We use this stable at rodeo time and during the agricultural show. During the show, we basically live here for a week.'

He took in the fairly primitive surroundings. 'Where do you sleep?'

'There's a loft upstairs.' She pointed to a ladder. 'It's luxury compared to a swag on hard ground.' She clapped her hands together. 'Right, let's see what you're made of, and if you can impress the girls.' She circled her arm, indicating the interested horses.

He growled in indignation. 'I always impress the girls.'

She arched her brows and wrinkled her button nose. 'Is that so?'

The challenge fizzed in her eyes, socking him in the chest. It was the first sign of blatant flirting he'd ever seen from her.

'So, you stand legs apart.' She adopted a wide stance. 'Put your weight on your left foot and then step your right diagonally forward like this.'

He copied her actions.

'Then you lock your left foot behind and step your right foot to the right. This is called wizard or Dorothy steps.'

'As in the Wizard of Oz?' He executed the basic steps.

'I suppose so. Now we do it all to the left and then again to the right.'

He danced the steps both left and right. 'This is pretty simple, and it's all to the count of eight?'

'You catch on fast, cowboy.' She flashed a wide smile, her white teeth gleaming in the low light.

His gut kicked over. 'What about the promenade?'

She quickly moved in front of him, her back pressing firmly against his front as she placed his right hand on her waist and held his left hand up above her shoulder.

Her heat instantly invaded his body, darting in deep and rippling out, before settling in his groin. He swallowed a groan.

She moved forward and he moved with her, and together they walked in a circle between the horse stalls. 'This is a square dancing position.' She twirled in his arms and came to face him, her hands resting palms down on his chest, her fingers splayed in proprietorial firmness.

Silver eyes gazed up at him from under thick brown lashes. 'Line-dancing is pretty much all about no-touch technique.'

The words washed over him, their sultry tone leaving little to be interpreted.

He met her gaze full on. 'Square dancing sounds like much more fun.'

'So why am I teaching you line-dancing?' Her arms snaked around his neck as she rose on the tips of her pink leather boots and kissed him.

Soft, luxurious lips closed over his, nipping at his bottom lip, firmly giving and demanding at the same time. White lights fired in his head.

He'd memorised the touch of her mouth but the reality of it outshone the memory, dimming it to a dull, flat grey.

For a few blissful moments he passively accepted the caresses, the kisses and the wonder of the sexiest mouth he'd ever known. But with each stroke of her tongue, with each nip of her teeth, his desire raged against his self-imposed restraint until it spilled over, hot and demanding.

He kissed her right back.

He tasted the spice of her perfume, the musk of desire and the simplicity of need.

He recognised that need. He knew it intimately.

With one gentle tug the pearl snap buttons on her blouse

opened and he gave thanks for the ease of western clothing. His hand touched fiery hot skin. As he nuzzled her neck, his fingers dealt with the more complicated issue of her bra fastening. The frothy lace finally gave way and ripe, heavy flesh rested where it belonged, in the curve of his hand.

It felt so right. His thumb caressed her breast, teasing her nipple to rise against his skin.

She gasped.

Pulling back slightly, she ripped open his shirt, pressing her lips against his chest, her tongue abrading his nipples.

He locked his knees for support as his blood pounded away from his head.

He gently gripped her head, raising her mouth back to his and then his hands caressed her breasts, kneading and stroking, until she sank against him, her moans of pleasure threatening his control.

Suddenly she pulled away, panting, her lips glistening and swollen and her eyes large black discs of pure lust. She'd never looked so beautiful.

The cool evening air rushed in against his bare chest, bringing his surroundings back into focus, and some sanity along with it.

This was Emily. His friend. His hand rubbed the back of his neck. 'What are we doing?' Somehow his voice managed to croak out the words.

She grabbed his hand. 'What we both want.'

He pulled her against him, staring hard into her eyes. 'This isn't a good idea.' He tried to make the words sound convincing as his body screamed in protest.

Her hand cupped his cheek. 'I think it's a perfect idea.'

He tugged at his hair. 'Are you sure this is what you want. I can't prom—'

She put her forefinger against his lips. 'Shh. It's all right. This time I know what I'm doing. I want this. One night is all I'm asking.'

'Em—'

Her mouth crushed his, filling him with her flavour of innocence and arousal.

Step back now! But the faint voice struggled to make itself heard against the pounding of his blood and the raging power of his desire for this incredibly sexy woman who stood in front of him.

As hard as it had been, he'd stepped back once before when she hadn't wanted him.

But this time she was offering.

Just one night.

This time he couldn't step back.

Somehow, on boneless legs they made it up the ladder to a mattress bedded down on hay. Emily knelt in front of him, her chin tilted, her shoulders back as she shrugged off her already open shirt and bra. The white soft glow of moonlight shone through the cracks of the corrugated iron, highlighting her alabaster skin, shadowing the curves of her body and making her look like a Florentine statue.

He gazed, mesmerised by the gift he had in front of him.

Then she smiled and reached for his belt.

In an instant he had her on her back. 'Sweetheart if you want this cowboy to perform at his best, he shucks his own pants.'

She laughed, her eyes dancing with wicked intent.

A sudden realisation of practicalities sounded through the fog of Linton's desire. 'I wasn't planning this. I don't have a condom.'

She stroked a finger down his chest, her voice suddenly serious. 'It's OK. I've been on the Pill for a very long time.'

Take her, she's yours. The last barrier of sense fell away and he lowered his head to hers, losing himself in her mouth, in the softness of her breasts, in the generosity of her body, which welcomed him like no other ever had.

Emily's hands gripped Linton's head as his mouth grazed across her body, lighting a fire of sensation that built in intensity with every stroke of his tongue. Nothing had prepared her for this. Not any of her fantasies, certainly not the controlling sex she'd known with Nathan. Nothing at all.

Pleasure morphed with pain. Her breasts ached with need, her legs quivered with longing, and a desperate emptiness inside her pleaded to be filled.

He paused for a moment, lifting his head, his eyes dark with arousal. He gently swept her hands up above her head. 'Sweetheart, I can't move if you immobilise my head. Lie back and enjoy, I want to give you this.'

'But I want you, I need you.' She whimpered the words on a ragged breath. She didn't care that she was pleading—nothing mattered except her need of him.

'Oh, my darling, you'll have me, don't worry about that.' He flashed a wicked grin and dropped his head between her legs.

She shattered at his touch, crying out his name as her body called for his.

He cradled her close, his whispered words promising her longed-for fulfilment. Then he eased inside her slowly, her muscles straining, and she felt his hesitation.

'No, don't stop.' Her hands clawed at his buttocks.

His eyes, full of caring, gazed down at her and then she moved against him, taking him, accepting all of him, driving them both to a place way beyond the stars.

She came back to earth piece by piece, completely reconfigured, a new Emily.

She lay snuggled in his arms, languorous and sated, but at the same time feeling more energised than she'd ever felt in her life.

She loved resting her head on his chest, hearing his heart beat strongly and rhythmically beneath her ear. Loved the way a trail of pale brown hair arrowed down his washboard flat abdomen, hinting at the power that lay at its destination.

And what a mighty power it was.

Linton was the most amazing lover. Not that she had vast experience to draw on, but from what he'd just shown her, she knew he was the man for her.

The *only* man for her.

Her stomach suddenly rolled.

Oh, God, she loved him.

No, this couldn't be happening. This was a one-night stand, a physical thing, pure lust, pure insanity. It was supposed to be the answer to her moving on—make love and get him out of her system.

But instead she'd fallen in love with a kind and generous man who had set her on the path of realising she could be whoever she wanted to be. A man who listened to her, took a great interest in her life and actively encouraged her to take risks, and at the same time acted as her safety net.

A man who only ever wanted one night. A man who didn't believe in for ever.

Leave now.

Shock drowned her. Nausea pulled at her and she breathed deeply, trying to settle her stomach. She couldn't be sick. Not here. Every part of her screamed to get away. She rolled from his side, sat up and pulled her shirt on.

He stirred and reached for her, his voice thick with post-coital relaxation. 'Hey, where are you going?'

She tugged on her boots before another spasm hit her, making her double over. 'Bathroom. Dodgy rodeo food.'

'Wait, I'll come with you.' He pushed a muscular arm through his shirtsleeve.

Her foot hit the top rung of the ladder, bile scalding her throat. 'Can't wait.'

'Emily!'

But she ignored his call, ignored the incredulity in his voice and she ran out of the stable and straight to the toilet block, her stomach surging.

Slamming the cubicle door behind her, she promptly vomited into the bowl.

The security guard outside the bank of women's portable toilets gave Linton a severe look. 'Can I help you, sir?'

Linton silently groaned. He'd been looking for Emily for ten minutes, quietly saying her name outside a few of the cubicles, trying not to draw attention to himself. What did you say to a security guard when you'd lost the woman you'd just had sex with?

'I'm waiting for someone.'

His brain spun. He'd just experienced some of the most amazing sex of his life and now Emily had disappeared. Part of him thought he must have imagined the whole thing. But he could still smell her perfume on his skin, and feel her hands on his body, taste her on his lips. It hadn't been a dream. It had been a glorious reality.

And lying with Emily for those few precious minutes with her warm body snuggled against his had been… He reached for a word but all he could come up with was 'perfect'. He frowned. That couldn't be the right word at all.

And then she'd rushed off.

Usually that's your role.

He stiffened against the thought and ran his hands through his hair. He needed to see her, needed to talk to her. Check she was OK, not just from food poisoning but also in other ways.

He started pacing. What had he just done? He'd let desire overrule every aspect of common sense. Emily wasn't a one-night sort of a girl. If he could just talk to her, check she was OK.

Make sure she has no expectations. The cynical voice pulled no punches.

He kicked the dirt, trying to kick the acrid thought away. No, he would take her out to dinner on a real date so they could firm up their friendship. Make sure it would survive tonight's madness.

A squeaky door opened and he spun around. A white-faced Emily appeared.

He instantly put his arm around her, worried she was about to fall over. 'You look shocking.'

She mustered a wry smile. 'Gee, you sure know how to make a girl feel good.'

He tucked stray curls hair behind her ear and whispered, 'I've never made a girl sick before.'

She patted his arm. 'No need to worry, your reputation is intact. I brought this on myself. I stupidly let that aroma of salt and deep-fried fat tempt me, and it makes me sick every time.' She sighed as contrition filled her face. 'Sorry. It wasn't the best way to end something that was pretty spectacular.'

'It was spectacular, wasn't it?' He grinned despite himself.

'But completely insane.' She wobbled against him.

He tilted her chin with his fingers, forcing her to look at him. 'Do you regret it?'

Shadows darkened her eyes before she quickly blinked several times. 'No, of course not.' Her words rushed out, tumbling over each other, almost too definite. 'It was my idea, remember? Just one night and this was it.'

The firmness of her voice should have reassured him. Instead, disquiet wove through him that he had trouble shrugging off.

She cleared her throat. 'I really need to go home to bed.'

'I'll take you.'

She pulled away from his touch. 'Dad's going to take me. I texted him.'

Her dismissal of him rankled. 'I would have happily taken you.'

She shrugged. 'You don't need a forty-minute drive in both directions.'

He should be relieved that she wasn't clingy, that she had no expectations of him. Instead, he had this crazy sensation of being discarded 'So…you'll be OK?'

She folded her arms across her chest. 'I'll be fine after some ginger tea and a long sleep.'

His skin prickled with frustration. 'I'll see you next week, then.'

She waved to her father and Stuart, who had just appeared in the distance. 'No, on Monday I leave for Sydney.'

Her soft words hit with the force of a punch. 'What do you mean, you'll be in Sydney?'

'I'm taking some annual leave to finish two assignments, as well as doing my residential week for my Master's. I'll be gone almost three weeks.'

All control seemed to be streaming away from him. 'Hang on, you can't just leave.'

She sighed and shook her head. 'Do you *ever* read your

memos, Linton? Cathy and Michael are back from their honeymoon so you'll have your old team back. You'll have a great
time and you won't even miss me.'

She turned and greeted her father. 'Sorry, Dad.'

Jim rolled his eyes. 'Honestly, Emily, you know you
shouldn't eat rodeo food. Come on, I'll take you home.' He
put his arm around his daughter's shoulder. 'Night all.'

''Night.' Linton watched them walk away with an inexplicable feeling of isolation.

Stuart clapped him on the shoulder. 'You any good at
pool?'

The question startled him. 'Fair, although your sister's
whipped me at it twice. Why?'

'Mark's off romancing the kinder teacher so the Tippett
team is one short. And I wouldn't worry about Em, she whips
most of us.'

He should say no. He should go home. This wasn't his
family. But his family had never offered him anything like this
sense of belonging. The feel-good flush at being included
overrode the amber caution light that started flashing in his
brain, telling him his inclusion in this family's life was getting
way too deep.

CHAPTER ELEVEN

SYDNEY'S unseasonably warm winter sun sparkled off the blue water of the harbour. Emily sat in the park at Circular Quay, admiring the architectural brilliance of the Opera House, the distinctive sails glowing white in the sunshine. Street theatre drew crowds, with young English and American backpackers doing feats of brilliance with fire and chain-saws, their engaging banter filling the air.

There was colour and movement, cosmopolitan sophistication, big city verve but, as much as she enjoyed it all, she was counting down the days until she returned to Warragurra.

Her mobile phone rang, the display unreadable in the bright sunlight. 'Hello, Emily Tippett.'

'Why aren't you in lectures?'

A deep voice tinged with mock seriousness rumbled down the line, warming her in places sunshine never could. She instantly smiled. 'Why are you ringing me if you think I won't answer?'

Linton had been calling and texting with increasing frequency during her time in Sydney. It had been the last thing she'd expected and it totally confused her. But she refused to dwell on that confusion. Instead, she lost herself in the sound of his voice.

He laughed. 'Good point. I should have texted you but I had a few minutes spare after a frantic morning.'

She heard the warbling of magpies over the phone and a wave of homesickness hit her. 'Where are you?'

'Down by the river.'

She pictured the gnarly river red gums lining the ancient watercourse, casting their much-needed shade over the often dry and dusty park.

'Where are *you*?'

His welcome voice broke into her thoughts. 'Outside the Museum of Contemporary Art.'

'Exactly what course are you studying?' His teasing warmth radiated down the phone. 'So will patients now be getting a dissertation on modernism in Australia as well as an ECG?'

She laughed, loving the buzz that vibrated inside her when they had these silly conversations. 'That's right. And I was thinking we need fluorescent gel for the ultrasound so we can create works of art on abdomens.'

'It has interesting possibilities. Of course, I think the professional approach would be to workshop it first.' His voice became husky. 'I'd happily donate my abdomen to the cause.'

The image of his flat, toned stomach flooded her mind. Her fingers tingled as if they could still feel the strength of it and her mouth recalled the salty taste. Puffs of heat spiralled through her and she had to force her voice to sound normal, rather than breathless, which it so wanted to be. 'I'll keep that in mind.'

His flirting was killing her but, tragic case that she was, she lived for his daily phone calls and his supportive texts, which seemed to pop up just when she thought her head would explode from too much academic jargon. He made her laugh and that in turn made her put her studies into perspective.

She dusted lint off her fine corduroy skirt. 'I just needed some air. I'm completely over having to apply theory to everyday things which are as much a part of me as breathing. I can't wait to come home.' *I can't wait to see you in person, even though it will only be at work.*

'Well, not long now. You're flying back on Saturday afternoon, right?'

'Yep, right in the middle of the grand final match.' She could hear her brothers groaning from here. 'Somehow I don't think familial devotion is so strong that the lads will abandon the match to collect me, so I'll bring my book and wait until half-time, when a taxi might take the chance at a fare.'

'I'll pick you up.'

The offer came instantly, shocking her, sending her blood to her feet. But at the same time buoying her up. 'Really? Are you sure? I wasn't dropping a hint.'

'Emily.' The stern doctor's voice had materialised.

She could imagine him rolling his eyes and shaking his head.

'It would be my pleasure to pick you up. It will be great to see you and, besides, I owe you dinner.'

'You do?'

'I do.' His voice was firm. 'I'll see you on Saturday, then. Bye.'

'Bye.' *I love you.* The unspoken words boomed in her head.

Suddenly a blast of energy whipped through her, urging her to deal with the final outstanding assignments required by the end of her residential week. Then she could head home. Home to Linton.

Hugging the thought close, she grabbed her backpack and jumped to her feet. The Opera House tilted sideways, the green grass at her feet spun upwards and her stomach flipped over and over before surging up to scald the back of her throat. She sat down heavily on the seat and waited for the spinning to stop.

She slowly blew out a breath to steady herself. That had been weird. Perhaps she was hungry? She rummaged through her bag, looking for a lolly or a muesli bar, something that would give her an instant sugar fix. Her fingers grasped a foil packet and she pulled it out, but it was only her contraceptive pill. She almost dropped it back in the bag but her fingers gripped it harder as she noticed she was about to start the hormone tablets again.

A rogue thought struck her. She should have had her period by now.

Her heart pounded hard against her ribs. She slowly counted backwards, her mind trying to race against her imposed thoroughness. She *always* started her period on the second day of the placebo tablets and she'd taken the seventh placebo last night.

Her roiling stomach plummeted to her feet. *No.* She couldn't be pregnant. She couldn't. She'd never missed a pill—she'd taken it every day at the same time for the three years since she'd gone on it to lessen period pain.

But you'd never had sex while on this brand of pill.

Her head fell into her hands as realisation slugged her. The night they'd made love she'd been sick, so even though she'd taken the pill, it hadn't stayed in her system long enough to do the job it had been designed to do.

It was a classic mistake. One she'd seen women make over and over.

Only she was a health professional. She knew better. She straightened up, holding onto that thought like a lifeline. The problem here was that she knew too much and she was jumping to silly conclusions. She wouldn't be pregnant—there would be some other much more reasonable explanation.

She threw her backpack over her shoulder and walked to the closest chemist, ignoring the wobbly sensation that had transferred from her stomach to her legs. On auto pilot she purchased a pregnancy test.

Five minutes later, in the spartan confines of a public toilet, she worried her bottom lip, her eyes glued to the stick in the little plastic cup.

Nothing was happening. She blew out a long-held breath. She'd just panicked and caused herself a heap of stress for nothing.

The timer on her watch sounded and she picked up the stick and cup, ready to dispose of them in the bin.

A faint blue colour slowly emerged, darkening before her eyes.

Pregnant.

She slumped against the cubicle wall. Oh, God, how had her life come to this?

Gulping in air, she tried to think clearly as a thousand thoughts charged around her head. She was going to be a mother. She was going to have a baby.

Linton's baby.

Sheer joy and abject fear collided in her chest.

It will be great to see you. I owe you dinner. Linton's deep, sexy voice bounced around her head. On the phone he'd sounded genuinely pleased that she was coming home.

Had he missed her? She delved in her pack and found her

phone. Flicking through her inbox, she counted and averaged that she'd received about two texts a day from him and she could only remember two or three days they hadn't spoken.

And he'd initiated all of it. Surely that meant something. It *had* to mean something.

Perhaps all his talk about never marrying again, never having children, were now empty words. Perhaps the playboy doctor had decided his playing days were over and he was ready to settle down.

I don't do long-term relationships and I won't ever let another women put me in that position. I will never get married again. His bitter words peppered her brain.

Darkness closed in on her. She loved this man and carried his child. It should be a wonderful, wonderful thing. But would he see it that way?

Plans and ideas popped into her head, things she could do, things that would make it easier for him, how she could lessen the impact, how she could...

Stop it! The tumbling thoughts abruptly stopped.

That would be a backward step. No, she had to stay true to herself and she knew what she had to do. She would return to Warragurra and tell him that she loved him, and that they were going to be parents.

Then she would ask him to marry her.

Linton scanned the wide blue skies, his hand shielding his eyes from the glare of a Warragurra sun, which hinted at the extreme heat that would arrive in a few months. Winter was fast coming to a close and the brilliant red of the flowering gums in the main street declared spring could not be stopped.

The airport was extremely quiet as the entire town was at the grand final, the Roosters having managed to turn around their form late in the finals. Team flags fluttered in the breeze, the distinctive maroon and yellow decorating everything that stood still at the airport and in the town.

He leaned against the waist-high cyclone fence, enjoying being on his own. Work had been busy but with Michael and Cathy back it had, as Emily had predicted, been very smooth.

But he'd missed Emily. Her sharp wit, her friendly smiles, her total absence of obsequiousness…

You missed her body, too.

He ran his hand across the back of his neck. He couldn't deny it. He missed her lingering perfume, the way his hand fitted in the small of her back when she passed through a doorway before him, and he missed the way her eyes sparkled when she smiled.

It was crazy but he felt cheated by the fact she'd rushed off to Sydney. Their *one night* had left him feeling short-changed because it hadn't been one night. It had been an hour.

But at the same time part of him had been worried that she would regret having given herself to him, that everything between them would have changed. However, over the phone she seemed to be the same Emily as the one he'd known before they'd made love.

His good mate.

He usually only made love with experienced women, never totally trusting a naïve 'just tonight' because they usually wanted a hell of a lot more from him.

Like Tamara had.

And Emily, despite her previous relationship, wasn't experienced. Women like Emily wanted home and hearth and a happy ever after.

He couldn't promise that to anyone.

But hearing her voice each day had helped allay his fears and she certainly hadn't sounded like she had any regrets. She'd obviously meant what she said.

Just one night, and this was it. The space under his ribs ached and he pressed against it, wondering if he should have a liver-function test as that ache had been bothering him lately.

He glanced at his watch. Three-thirty. The plane should be here soon and he and Emily could spend the rest of the afternoon and evening together. He'd decided against dinner at the Royal as the grand final crowd would be in full swing.

Instead, he was really looking forward to taking Emily home to dinner and being able to sit across from her when he talked to her rather than imagining if her cute nose was wrinkling or if her hands were busy gesticulating, talking for her as much as her mouth.

He had so much to tell her. Jason had finally managed to master suturing and she'd appreciate what a momentous achievement that was, whereas Cathy had just looked bemused at the high-fives.

The buzz of the Beech Baron's propellers sounded before he sighted the white, five-seater plane. Five minutes later its wheels touched down and it taxied to a stop. The pilot jumped out of the cockpit, pulled down the steps and opened the plane's door.

Two men and a woman appeared and then Emily stood in the doorway, her flyaway curls fire-engine red.

His gut kicked in alarm. What the hell was wrong? But then she smiled and waved and he realised she'd probably just missed Warragurra. He was learning her hair was like an emotional universal indicator, going as many colours as the paper strips in the chemistry lab. The country girl must have tired of the city.

He strode out to meet her, his eyes only for her, when he heard a loud, familiar male voice sound from behind her.

'Linton, I thought I'd surprise you. Lucky for me this young lady seems to know you.' Bushy eyebrows rose in a lecherous look. 'I can see why you're enjoying small-town life.'

His father stood next to Emily, his hand on the small of her back, guiding her in front of him.

Linton's stomach fell to his feet. Of all the days his father could have chosen to have one of his frequent but unan-nounced visits, this wasn't his best choice. His quiet dinner with Emily evaporated before his eyes. 'Dad.' He extended his hand. 'Good to see you.'

'You're still welcome for dinner.' Linton hauled Emily's bag out of the boot of his car as the farm dogs barked in joyous glee at seeing Emily again.

Emily smiled a tired smile. 'We can do it another time. You head back to town and catch up with your dad.'

Linton slammed the boot closed. 'He does this. Just turns up unannounced for a few days. It's usually when he's between girlfriends.'

'He's probably lonely.' Grey shadows hovered under her eyes and exhaustion hung over her in complete contrast to her usual bubbly style. On the journey out to the station she'd been interested in his conversation but he'd sensed an unusual reserve. Something that hadn't been present in their phone calls.

'Dad's hardly lonely.' But he noticed she hadn't heard his words.

She stood gazing out across Woollara's home-paddock garden, out toward the shearing shed, breathing in deeply. 'It's great to be home.'

She took a tentative step forward, stopped and then gave a self-conscious laugh.

He grinned at the glimpse of a young girl in her face. 'What?'

Her eyes sparkled. 'It will sound silly but when I've been away I usually go and visit the river, and say, "Hello, I'm back."'

He extended his hand, not wanting to leave her just yet. 'Let's go together. I could do with a walk.'

'Thank you. That would be lovely.' Her face broke into a smile that encompassed her entire body, totally vanquishing the tiredness that clung to her.

It was like being showered in golden light, and heat spiralled through him, warming him at first before stoking into a fiery blaze.

Her hand touched his and he pulled her into his arms to placate muscles that had ached to hold her. His lips hungrily sought hers, desperate to taste her, desperate to brand her with his own taste.

She responded instantly, her arms wrapping themselves around his neck, her body moulding itself to his, her lips kissing him until his need for breath made him draw away regretfully.

She laughed as he regained his breath, her arm around his waist. 'I take it that you missed me.'

He slid his arm around her shoulders and started walking toward the river, dropping a light kiss on the top of her head. 'I did.'

The two sheepdogs raced in front of them, before quickly turning and racing away again.

She glanced up at him, her grey eyes serious. 'That's good, because I really missed you.'

A muscle in his neck tightened and he tried laughter to release it. 'So that's why your hair's scarlet.'

She stumbled against him before finding her footing again. 'Partly.'

The softness of her voice sent a streak of discomfort through him. He'd expected her to deny it; he'd expected her to say it was the agonies of having to study nursing theory, the stress of getting two large assignments completed in a short space of time.

They walked the last hundred metres to the riverbank in contemplative silence. She broke away from him and caught the swinging rope that hung from the large gumtree by the side of the waterhole. Her eyes took on a far-away stare. 'I loved swinging off this rope when I was a kid. We'd all come down here and Mum would cook sausages and Dad would be the biggest kid of us all, bombing us as he let go of the rope.' She turned toward him. 'Where did you swim?'

He put his hands gently on her shoulders, the need to touch her, to be connected to her paramount. 'Dad had a pool.' He thought of the times he'd swum there alone, in stark contrast to the scene she'd just depicted.

She stepped in close and unexpectedly dropped her head on his chest as a shudder trembled through her.

The shudder built on his own unease. He ran his hand down her cheek. 'Emily, what's going on?'

She bit her lip and dragged in a breath, tilting her head to look up at him, joy and hesitancy filling her gaze. 'Um, there's no easy way to say this so I just will. We're pregnant.'

Blood pounded loud in his ears as his breath stalled in his lungs. *Pregnant! A child, their child.* For an instant a fuzzy image of a child on his knee and Emily's arms around his neck played through his brain, bringing warmth and a sense of belonging.

Never let yourself get trapped, like I did, son. His father's mantra exploded in his head, driving away the fragile image. Confusion swamped him. He put his hands on her forearms, lifting her slightly away from him. 'How? How can you be pregnant?'

She smiled at him like he was a child himself. 'Three weeks ago we had a pretty intense moment in the loft at the stables.'

Irritation skated through him at her smile. 'I know how babies are made, Emily. But you said you were on the Pill. You said you were protected.'

An anguished look crossed her face. 'I told you the truth, Linton. But when I got sick it mucked up the hormone levels and I didn't even think because it had been such a long time since I'd…'

Made love. He needed to move, he needed to think. He dropped his hands from hers and raked them through his hair. 'Hell, what a mess. Two health professionals who should have known better, with an unwanted pregnancy.'

'It's not unwanted.' Her quiet words sliced deeply through him, like the blade of a surgeon's scalpel. 'I want to have *our* baby very much.'

His head snapped up to meet her gaze. Love shone from silver eyes, pure and all-encompassing. Like a fist to the gut, white pain winded him. His legs threatened to crumple underneath him.

She loves me.

Emily stood before him, loving him and pregnant with his child.

His worst nightmare encircled him, binding him with its tendrils of responsibility and commitment. He didn't want to get married again. He didn't want to be a father. He didn't want to be loved.

He started to pace, his brain slowly emerging from the fog of shock. 'This should never have happened. Getting married for the sake of the child doesn't work. I'm living proof of that. We'll share custody and I'll support you and the child financially.'

Her shoulders stiffened and suddenly she seemed taller. 'So just like that you'll deny your child a loving home.'

Her accusing words stung. 'No, I will not deny this child anything. He will have two loving homes. Yours and mine.' He stared her down. 'It worked for me.'

'Oh, yeah, right, and you're such an emotional rock.' Derision slashed across her face. 'Children need two parents in the same house.'

Memories of his early years pounded in his head and he heard himself yelling, 'Not if the parents are going to tear each other apart.'

'So you're not even prepared to try?'

It took every ounce of his willpower to ignore the disgust in her voice. 'I know it wouldn't work.'

She stepped in close, her scent encircling him, her hand resting gently on his arm. 'I know this is a shock and that you're scared. I'm scared too but sometimes the best things in life require a huge risk.'

Her soft voice continued, like balm to the chaos in his head. 'We're not your parents. We are not you and Tamara. We have a chance. We laugh together, we work together well, we're really good friends—we can do this. We can be a happy family.' Hope shone from her eyes, driven by love.

For the first time in weeks the space under his ribs stopped throbbing.

But then, like the roar of a cyclone, voices suddenly detonated in his head, exploding Emily's words. *Don't make the same mistake twice, son.* Tamara's whining voice chased his father's. *You've made my life miserable.*

He lifted Emily's hand from his arm. 'But friendship isn't love and without that we'll destroy each other. I watched my parents do that. I lived it with Tamara. My father's right. It's not a risk I'm prepared to take again.'

Her shocked gasp sounded as painful as if he'd struck her across the face. He hated it that he'd hurt her but one of them had to be rational. One of them had to see sense, skirt the emotional minefield that would inevitably blow up in their faces.

She slumped against the tree but then she jutted her chin out, eyes blazing. 'You told me that Tamara didn't love you so of course your marriage failed, how could it not? And did it ever occur to you that your father is wrong? That by listening to his jaundiced view you can't recognise love when it's staring you in the face.' She threw her arms up, her face suddenly hard and determined.

'So go live in your safe little controlled world where you don't have to risk a thing,' she said. 'You once told me that I was never true to myself. Well, I've grown up. You obviously don't want this child but I do. He'll have four uncles and a grandfather that will love him to bits, and that will have to be enough.'

She stepped away from the tree. 'Go back to Sydney and take your financial support with you. I don't want it.' Spinning on her heel, she ran up the bank, back toward the homestead, back toward her home.

'Emily!' He called her name but she didn't stop.

And what would he say if she did stop? He couldn't offer her what she wanted. He couldn't accept what she offered. It was a no-win situation.

A sigh shuddered out of him, generated from the depths of his soul. As hard as it seemed right now, she'd come to see he was right.

And he knew he was right.

He inhaled sharply as the space under his ribs burned hot and raw.

CHAPTER TWELVE

LINTON longed to go home. He'd even settle for a medical emergency to pull him back to the hospital, not that he'd wish ill health on anyone. Since his father's arrival twenty-four hours ago they'd been to the huge grand final party at the Royal, played golf that morning and now he was saddle sore from playing polo. His father had seen Penelope's invitation and had insisted they attend.

This was his father's modus operandi every time he visited—socialising non-stop.

Warragurra was too small to avoid running into Emily's family but so far he'd managed a distant wave in the crush at the Royal and the same today with Nadine and Hayden. Dealing with that uncomfortable reality would come soon enough. Sadness settled over him. He'd enjoyed the friendship of the brothers.

'You played well.' Penelope's voice purred as she handed him a glass of champagne.

He clinked her glass. 'Thanks. I'm a bit rusty.'

She stared at him brazenly, her eyes hungry. 'You looked pretty good to me.'

He ignored the comment and took another sip of champagne. Any other time he would have taken the flirting bait.

He would have linked his arm with hers, told her she looked stunning, complimented her on her natty new handbag and strolled with her toward an evening that would have finished with the two of them in bed.

She raised her perfectly waxed eyebrows. 'Where have you been hiding yourself lately?'

Emily's face washed through his mind. He steeled himself against the sensation of loss that seemed to grow inside him every time he thought about her. 'Work's been busy.'

'Too much work makes Linton a dull boy.' The pout of her mouth closed around the fine glass flute.

Exasperation flared inside him. He was a doctor, for heaven's sake. Doctors by the nature of their jobs worked hard. He'd never had to explain that to Emily, she just knew. She understood.

'That's what I've been telling him.' Peter Gregory's voice boomed beside him as he stepped up next to Penelope.

'But sons never listen to their fathers.' Pen appraised his father's expensive casual clothes, his hand-made Italian shoes, his trendy Sydney haircut and his designer watch. 'You look too young to be Linton's father.'

Peter's chest puffed out and Linton braced himself for the line he'd heard all his life.

'Well, I'm more like an older brother than a father.'

Peter extended his hand toward Penelope. 'Peter Gregory, seeing as Linton's a little slow on the introductions.'

She seized his hand. 'Penelope Grainger. Lovely to meet you.'

'And you. I must say that shade of pink suits you perfectly, but, then, I'm sure you could model any designer's clothes to their advantage.'

Linton cringed and quickly downed the last mouthful of

his champagne. What was his father thinking? Penelope was too young for him.

Penelope's hand fluttered at her throat. 'Peter, would you like to watch the next chukka with me?'

Peter slipped his arm through hers. 'That sounds delightful.'

As they strolled off, Peter turned back toward Linton and winked.

Linton knew that wink. It meant the game was on and he thought he was in with a chance.

His blood suddenly dropped to his feet and white noise buzzed loudly in his head as reality hit him. He was his father. Hell, he even acted like his father, using the same lines, the same mannerisms.

His stomach churned, the champagne burning and fizzing as his future rolled out before him and he hated the way it looked.

Did it ever occur to you that your father is wrong? Emily's pointed question hit him between the eyes. He sagged against the pole of the marquee, needing the support it offered.

For the first time in his life he'd just seen his father for who he truly was.

A very lonely, emotionally shallow, fifty-two-year-old man.

A man who'd never enjoyed a successful adult relationship because he rejected every woman before they'd got close to him. A man who had never known a soulmate.

He forced air down into his lungs against the tightness constricting his chest. He didn't want to end up like his father. He wanted more out of life than that.

We have a chance. Emily's voice sounded through the swirling mess that was his mind. All this time he'd thought that, by committing to Emily and the baby, he was being trapped.

But, in fact, he was being rescued.

Oh, God. What had he done? Yesterday he'd sent away the best thing that had ever happened to him. He'd rejected Emily's love and he'd rejected his one chance at real happiness.

He loved her. She was his soulmate.

The realisation slugged into him so hard his legs trembled.

'Are you all right, sir?' An anxious waiter hovered.

The words cut through his shock and bewilderment. 'I'm fine. There's just something I have to do.'

He ran from the marquee straight to his car. He'd drive direct to Woollara, straight to Emily.

He only hoped she would forgive him.

Emily had finished the rosters, completed the stock order for the supply room, scrubbed the pan room and now she'd run out of things to do. Sunday afternoon in A and E could be frantic but today, when she needed to be busy, it had failed to deliver.

Technically, she wasn't even due back until Monday but she'd reworked the rosters, making sure she worked most weekends and afternoon shifts. That way she would see a lot less of Linton and work more with Daniel and Michael.

Mostly she just wanted to run back to the Flying Doctors but she had an obligation to work out a two-week resignation period and she wasn't going to leave abruptly and end up looking petty.

Once she was back working with the Flying Doctors, she wouldn't run into Linton very much at all. And then he'd be gone, back to Sydney, where he belonged.

The aching sadness inside her grew with every passing minute. She pulled the calendar off the wall, counting how many weeks Linton still had left in Warragurra. She closed her eyes against the evidence. It was months. He'd leave around the time she'd commence maternity leave.

Maternity leave. It all seemed so surreal. She was going to be a mother. She hadn't mentioned the pregnancy to her family yet—it was all too new, too raw. Emotionally she wasn't ready to tell them because her brothers would probably go ballistic. She grimaced. Linton might decide it would be safer to leave Warragurra early after all.

And her dad? How would he react when he found out his little girl had got herself knocked up? She hoped he'd do what he often did when faced with big dilemmas. He'd hug her briefly and then get practical.

Well, she needed practical. Juggling a baby and full-time shift work would be…impossible? She shook herself. It had to be possible, she had no choice.

'Em.'

She turned to see her father gripping the edge of the nurses' station, his face a deathly grey.

'Dad?' She shot to her feet, terror gripping her. She grabbed a wheelchair, and pushed it behind him.

He fell into it, groaning. 'Hurts.' He gripped his chest and his lower abdomen with both arms.

'Jason.' She called the medical student, who'd been studying in the staffroom.

He appeared immediately. 'What's wrong?

'Ring Michael now! Tell him it's my father.' She pushed the wheelchair quickly into the resus room. 'Dad, can you get up onto the trolley if I help you?'

Beads of sweat lined Jim's forehead as he gasped for breath. 'I…drove…here so…I…can…do that.'

She locked the chair and, putting one foot between her

father's and one on the outside of his leg, placed her arms under his armpits and heaved.

Jim stumbled to his feet and together they shuffled around until his bottom touched the trolley.

She swung his legs up on the trolley and pulled off his boots, terrified by how her usually stoic and in-control father was dwarfed by this pain.

'Where does it hurt, Dad?' She fitted him with nasal oxygen.

'Everywhere.' He slumped against the pillows, sweaty and ashen, his face streaked with fear. 'I'm dying, aren't I?'

'Not today.' Her words sounded more confident than she felt. She flicked on the ECG machine, her fingers fumbling with the packaging that held the dots. She applied the dots with shaking fingers. *Where was Michael?* She calculated the amount of time it should take him to arrive at the hospital from his house.

Hurry up! She needed her dad. Her baby needed his granddad. She couldn't do motherhood without him.

Jason walked through the door. 'Doctor's on his way.' He gently took the leads from her numb fingers and connected them. Staring past her at the screen, he confidently announced, 'Sinus rhythm, elevated rate.'

Relief rushed through her. It wasn't a heart attack.

The door swung open. 'Jim, you look lousy.' Linton strode into the room, his mud-splattered polo whites outlining his long, strong legs. He tossed his quilted leather vest onto a chair and rolled up his royal-blue sleeves. 'Where does it hurt?'

Emily struggled to breathe. Fear for her father tripped over her shock at seeing Linton. Every painful moment of their conversation twenty-four hours ago reverberated in her head. He'd rejected her and in doing so he'd rejected her family.

'Michael is my father's doctor.' The words whipped out of her mouth, harsh and uncompromising.

His jaw stiffened, as if he'd been punched, but he reached for a stethoscope as he barked at Jason, 'Obs?'

She turned on the hapless Jason. 'I specifically told you to ring Michael.'

Jason blushed bright red. 'I—'

'I don't care who the hell looks after me—just take the pain away.'

Her father's anguished voice grounded her. 'Sorry, Dad.' She shot Linton a blistering look but the expected satisfaction from such an act didn't come.

Instead, he met her gaze, his eyes flickering with something akin to an apology. She quickly looked away and assisted her father into a gown so he could be examined.

'When did the pain start?' Linton's focus was one hundred per cent on Jim as he tapped the man's abdomen.

'I got a twinge a couple of hours ago just after I'd arrived in town for the historical society's meeting.' He flinched as he leaned forward. 'I think I'm going…to be…'

Jason thrust a bowl under Jim's chin as the grazier vomited into the bowl.

'He needs fluids.'

Linton's concerned voice tore at the fragile scab on Emily's heart. How could he come in here and act all worried and caring for her father when he couldn't love her or their baby?

Emily hung up the primed IV that Jason had prepared and then slipped a tourniquet around her father's arm. 'I'm just going to put in a drip, Dad.'

'I'll do it for you.' Linton ripped open an alcohol swab, his face stern and unyielding.

'That won't be necessary. I can do it.' She spoke through gritted teeth, the cannula box in her hand. She didn't want his help.

Jim glanced between the two of them and tilted his head toward Jason. 'I want the lad to do it.'

Jason hesitantly stepped forward, putting his hand out for the equipment.

'If that's what you want, Jim.' Linton gave a rueful smile and passed the swab to Jason.

Surprise rocked her. She hadn't expected him to capitulate to her father's request. Or let Jason execute the task.

'We'll give you morphine for the pain, Dad.' She clipped a drug chart under the clip of the chart board and handed it to Linton.

'Are you allergic to anything, Jim?' Linton pulled out his pen. 'Can you take pethidine?'

'Both are opiates, aren't they?' His face contorted in agony. 'Either one will do as long as it…stops…the…pain.' He closed his eyes, clearly exhausted. 'Do you always contradict each other?'

'I just want what's best for you, Dad.' Emily's frustration pumped though her as she checked the dose of pethidine with Jason. It was bad enough that her father was so ill, without having to deal with Linton.

'Linton will do that. Go wait outside.' Her father patted her arm.

'Ah, Jim, I need Emily here, so if you can go back to being the patient, that would really help.' Linton winked at Emily as he listened to Jim's chest.

Her heart bled a little more. Her father was treating her like a child, and Linton should be behaving like the low-life he was, but instead he was completely understanding and being kind.

None of it made any sense.

She injected the pethidine into the rubber bung on the IV line, knowing that within a minute it would act, easing her father's pain.

Jim suddenly gripped his lower back. 'Here. The pain's here but it goes all the way around the front and down here.' He pressed his groin area.

'He's got a temperature of 39.2.' Jason read the display on the ear thermometer.

'Renal colic.'

She spoke at the very same moment as Linton.

He smiled at her and nodded, his eyes full of warmth and adoration.

She staggered under the gaze. How could he look at her like that and yet tell her he couldn't love her?

'Well, it's good to see you two finally working together.' Jim's opiate-induced, glassy eyes stared at them both. He turned to Jason. 'Do they normally misbehave?'

Jason's mouth opened and shut, stunned at the question, unsure if he should answer it. 'Um, usually they're a team, Mr Tippett.'

'Well, of course they are.' Jim relaxed against the pillow. 'Had a lovers' tiff, did you?'

'Dad!' Emily's face burned with embarrassment and indignation pounded through her, despite the fact she knew it was the drug talking.

Jim grinned at Linton. 'I always found it worked best to say sorry, son. Oh, and flowers and chocolates never go astray either.'

Jason's eyes enlarged, incredulous at the conversation.

Linton seemed to choke on laughter. 'I'll keep that in mind, Jim. Meanwhile, hopefully, with the analgesia relaxing you,

you'll pass the kidney stone that has been giving you so much grief. I'll start you on antibiotics and we'll monitor your urine output, but right now the best thing for you to do is sleep.'

He turned to the stunned Jason. 'Mr Tippett is your patient, Jason. Do half-hourly observations, strain all urine and call us if there is any change.'

'Yes, Dr Gregory.' Jason stood a little taller.

'Emily, I need to talk to you.'

The supplication in Linton's voice battered at all her defences but she needed to stand firm. 'I need to stay with Dad.'

'No, you don't. I've got Jason looking after me.' Jim mumbled, 'Go and sort out whatever it is you need to sort out. Your mother and I never let the sun set on an argument.'

Emily sighed. Her father had *no idea* that the argument that lay between Linton and herself was insoluable. When two people wanted opposite things, resolution was unreachable.

She wasn't sure she had the strength to rehash the same arguments. But her father wasn't going to let her stay so she kissed him on the cheek and left the room.

She marched straight to the desk, opened her father's history and started to write up the nursing notes.

'That can wait.' Linton's quiet words sounded behind her. 'Come and have a cup of coffee.'

She spun around. 'Coffee makes me nauseous.'

'Ginger tea, then.'

She expected him to smile, the way he always did when he aimed to get his own way. Instead, his expression looked almost sad.

'Please, Emily.'

She could have resisted his smile. She could have stood resolute against the charm. But his complete lack of artifice disarmed her.

'All right.' She walked to the staffroom, each step filling her with dread.

He filled two cups with boiling water from the rapid-boil urn and jiggled a ginger teabag through one and regular tea though the other. He sat down on the couch next to her, handing her the cup.

'Thank you.'

'You're welcome.'

Stifling politeness expanded between them like a bubble. It was hard to believe that they had once reached for each other with such passionate need that everything else had faded to insignificance.

He cleared his throat. 'Michael rang me because his car wouldn't start.'

She nodded, resignation sliding through her. Was this their future? One of excessive politeness and treading with extreme caution?

'But I would have wanted to be here anyway. I have enormous respect for your father, he's a good man.' He delivered the words to the opposite wall.

She put down her tea, the drink far too hot at the moment. 'Well, that's good to know.' She couldn't hide the sarcasm from her voice. 'I'm not sure he's going to feel quite the same way about you.'

She wanted the barb to sting, to wound, to hurt him as much as he'd hurt her.

He flinched. 'I deserved that.' Putting his cup down on the side table, he turned to face her, his eyes dark with indecipherable emotions. 'Yesterday I behaved abysmally and I'm sorry.'

Exhaustion hit her as she realised why he wanted to talk to her. To give her a hollow apology. 'Are you here for absolution? Because if you are, I don't think I'm the right person to give it to you.'

He ran his hand across the back of his neck. 'I've been the biggest fool on earth.'

She didn't want to recognise the penitence on his face or hear the sorrow in his voice. 'You won't get an argument from me.'

He struggled to smile. 'You never let me get away with anything, Emily, and that is one of the many reasons why I love you.'

Her ears heard the words but her brain struggled to compute them. 'You love me?' The disbelief in her voice roared in her ears.

He reached for her hands, his palm closing over her knuckles with a touch so gentle it was as if he thought she might break. 'I love you. I'm sorry it took me so long to work it out.'

'But…but yesterday you told me you couldn't love me.' Her heart pounded so hard she could hear it in her head. Incredulity fought with want and need as she searched his face, looking for clues to solve this abrupt turnaround.

Pain slashed his face. 'If I could take back yesterday, take back all the hurtful things I said, then I would. You were right. I had no idea what love really is.'

'But you do now?' A bubble of hope slowly rose from her pit of despair. She wanted to believe him but she couldn't, not yet.

'I do now.' His deep voice vibrated with feeling. 'I love you so much it hurts.'

Hope sped through her. 'I know how that feels.' She bit her lip, trying to understand. 'But what happened to change your mind?'

He leaned in close. 'Dad.'

'Your father told you to marry me?' She couldn't stop the incredulity in her voice.

He shook his head. 'No. Dad doesn't know anything about you and me. Yet. But he soon will.' He rested his head on her forehead. 'This afternoon at the polo, it was like the scales fell from my eyes.'

His breath caressed her face. 'You were right, totally and utterly correct. My father is wrong about relationships. They don't trap people—they release love.'

Her heart tumbled over with joy. 'You really do love me?'

'I really do love you.'

He pulled her into his arms, kissing her hard and fast, making her feel giddy with wonder and bliss.

Then he cuddled her close. 'I'm so sorry it took me so long to realize that. All my life my father told me that marriage was a nightmare. I'd lived with my parents long enough to believe it and I hadn't managed to make a success of it with Tamara.'

He gripped her hands more firmly. 'Believing Dad absolved me of my ever risking my heart again. Except I lost it to you without even knowing.'

She cupped his cheek with her hand. 'I think I lost my heart to you the first day I met you.'

His eyes sparkled with elation. 'You've taken me on a wondrous journey, shown me how amazing a loving family can be and completed me in every way. You're my best friend. I didn't recognise that our friendship was love.'

'It's love of the strongest kind.'

He nodded his agreement. 'And our baby will grow up basking in our love and the love of your family. A grandchild might even soften up the old man.' He hesitated. 'That is, if you'll marry me.'

Sheer joy and happiness exploded inside her and she smiled a wide smile. 'Are you asking me?'

He slid off the couch, kneeling on a muddy knee. 'Emily Tippett, love of my life, mother of my child and future children, will you marry me?'

She looked into his earnest face, full of love, tinged with a sliver of doubt, and threw herself into his arms. Her lips touched his and she knew she was home.

She's forgiven me. Relief surged through Linton, quickly overtaken by all-encompassing happiness. She tasted so good he never wanted to let her go. 'I take it that's a yes.'

She nodded, her eyes dancing.

He pulled her to her feet. 'Let's go and tell your dad.'

She laughed. 'What, you think in his pethidine haze he'll give you permission to marry his only daughter?'

He slipped his arm around her waist and grinned. 'That's my plan.'

They walked along the corridor, her fingers snaking inside the gaps between the buttons on his shirt. 'You do realise he'll ask you how you're going to provide for me and where we're going to live.'

He paused outside the resus room door, twirling one of her crazy red curls around his finger. 'I guess we need to talk about that. I've always seen Sydney as the place I'd return to.'

Her commitment to him shone in her eyes. 'I'll come to Sydney if that's what you want, as long as I have a month at Woollara a couple of times a year so the baby knows his country heritage.'

The strength of her love made him dizzy. 'Or her heritage.'

'Either way.'

He gazed into her eyes, amazed at how long-held plans

could change without a murmur of regret. 'Except that I think our children deserve to grow up with their granddad teaching them to ride horses and their cousins teaching them to shell peas and climb trees.'

Her gasp of delight was reflected in the joy on her face. 'So you'd settle here in Warragurra?'

'I think you and I belong in Warragurra.' He lowered his lips to hers and kissed her.

Time stood still. Nothing existed but his lips on hers, the comfort of her arms, the wondrous touch of her body pressed hard against his and the promise of a future together.

'Hey, sis, there are sick people in this joint. Do you want to make them feel worse?'

He looked up to see Eric leading the rest of the Tippett family into the department. Holding Emily close to his side, all he could do was grin.

Emily giggled.

'It's about time.' Hayden, with Tyler on his shoulders, thumped Linton on the back before exchanging a knowing look with Nadine.

Mark smiled quietly at both of them, his face full of approval.

Stuart grinned. 'We've got a back-up member for the Tippett pool team.'

'You'd have to be desperate,' Emily teased. 'But he's got other skills.' She laid her hand possessively on his chest.

'So the flowers did the trick, Linton?' Jim's voice called as everyone walked into the room.

Emily reached up on tiptoe and pulled Linton's head down close to hers, her eyes sparkling with joy. 'Are you sure about this, about living in Warragurra? My family can be pretty full on.'

He glanced around, feeling all the love in the room. 'I wouldn't have it any other way.'

And he kissed her all over again.

Possessed by a passionate sheikh

The Sheikh's Bartered Bride by **Lucy Monroe**

After a whirlwind courtship, Sheikh Hakim bin
Omar al Kadar proposes marriage to shy
Catherine Benning. After their wedding day,
they travel to his desert kingdom, where
Catherine discovers that Hakim has bought her!

Sheikh's Honour by **Alexandra Sellers**

Prince and heir Sheikh Jalal was claiming all that
was his: land, title, throne…and a queen. Though
temptress Clio Blake fought against the bandit
prince's wooing like a tigress, Jalal would not be
denied his woman!

Available 19th September 2008

From international
bestselling author
EMMA DARCY

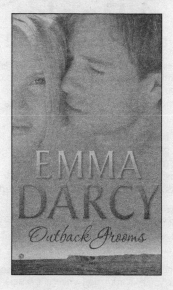

These three Outback bad boys are now rich, powerful
men – and they've come to claim their brides!

The Outback Marriage Ransom
The Outback Wedding Takeover
The Outback Bridal Rescue

Available 19th September 2008

www.millsandboon.co.uk

M&B

FREE!

4 Books
and a surprise gift!

We would like to take this opportunity to thank you for reading this Mills & Boon® book by offering you the chance to take FOUR more specially selected titles from the Medical™ series absolutely FREE! We're also making this offer to introduce you to the benefits of the Mills & Boon® Book Club—

- ★ **FREE home delivery**
- ★ **FREE gifts and competitions**
- ★ **FREE monthly Newsletter**
- ★ **Exclusive Mills & Boon Book Club offers**
- ★ **Books available before they're in the shops**

Accepting these FREE books and gift places you under no obligation to buy, you may cancel at any time, even after receiving your free shipment. Simply complete your details below and return the entire page to the address below. You don't even need a stamp!

YES! Please send me 4 free Medical books and a surprise gift. I understand that unless you hear from me, I will receive 6 superb new titles every month for just £2.99 each, postage and packing free. I am under no obligation to purchase any books and may cancel my subscription at any time. The free books and gift will be mine to keep in any case.

M8ZEF

Ms/Mrs/Miss/Mr ....Initials...................................
BLOCK CAPITALS PLEASE
Surname ....
Address...

....
....Postcode ....

Send this whole page to:
UK: FREEPOST CN81, Croydon, CR9 3WZ